The

PRINCE

of

NANTUCKET

Also by Jan Goldstein

All That Matters

The

PRINCE

of

NANTUCKET

a novel

JAN GOLDSTEIN

THREE RIVERS PRESS · NEW YORK

Copyright © 2007 by Jan Goldstein

Discussion Questions copyright © 2008 by Three Rivers Press,
an imprint of the Crown Publishing Group,
a division of Random House, Inc.

Published in the United States by Three Rivers Press, an imprint of the
Crown Publishing Group, a division of Random House, Inc., New York.
www.crownpublishing.com

Three Rivers Press and the Tugboat design are registered trademarks
of Random House, Inc.

Originally published in hardcover in the United States
by Shaye Areheart Books, an imprint of the Crown Publishing Group,
a division of Random House, Inc., New York, in 2007.

Library of Congress Cataloging-in-Publication Data
Goldstein, Jan.
The prince of Nantucket : a novel / Jan Goldstein.—1st ed.
1. Political candidates—Family relationships—Fiction.   2. Self-actualization
(Psychology)—Fiction.   3. United States. Congress. Senate—
Elections—Fiction.   4. Nantucket (Mass.)—Fiction.   I. Title.
PS3607.O4844P75 2007
813'.6—dc22   2006034256

ISBN 978-0-307-34591-2

Printed in the United States of America

Design by Lynne Amft

10 9 8 7 6 5 4 3 2 1

First Paperback Edition

For my wife, Bonnie—

Partner in life,
the world of dreams,
and many a Nantucket adventure.

She makes all things possible.

I carry your heart. I carry it in my heart.
—e. e. cummings

Acknowledgments

Writing novels is inevitably seen as a lonely vocation, a sole endeavor involving countless hours spent by oneself, staring at a computer screen or a legal pad, reworking a sentence, fashioning plot and characters into a (hopefully) cohesive whole. And while, from my experience, the veracity of that view is incontrovertible, it is equally true that few novels are produced without significant accomplices.

I am, as ever, indebted to my friend and agent, Linda Chester. She continues to provide both essential counsel and a plethora of encouragement in guiding my career. And she does it all with such grace and class. She is a remarkable woman. Gary Jaffe, the executive manager of Linda's office, is without peer, assisting me on numerous occasions with a wealth of patience, good humor, and genuine care. He is a gem.

I phoned author Chris Bohjalian about Shaye Areheart when she first expressed interest in this novel. His praise was earnest and effusive. I now know why. Both as an editor and a publisher, Shaye is extraordinary. She loves writers and, even more important, she has a unique passion for what they do. I discovered that her incisive skill in guiding and polishing a manuscript is matched by the heart and mind of an incredible human being.

I would like to thank the people at Random House, and more to the point, Crown, and in even finer detail, Shaye Areheart Books (it's a big family); they have all taken this novel to their hearts and helped bring it out into the world with professionalism and dedication. Jenny Frost (president and publisher of Crown) fell in love with the manuscript after a first reading. I greatly appreciate her strong support. My thanks to Kira Stevens, whose enthusiasm in marketing this novel is infectious, along with her colleagues Philip Patrick and Donna Passannante. I am most appreciative for the important contributions of Karin Schulze and Linda Kaplan (rights), Sibylle Kazeroid (production editor), Whitney Cookman (art director), and Jill Flaxman and all who are part of her dynamic sales force, which has gone all out to get this novel into readers' hands. Thanks also to Shaye's assistant, Anne Berry, for handling many of my queries and needs with aplomb. Finally, my deep gratitude to Christine Aronson and Tina Constable in Publicity and especially my publicist, the indefatigable Campbell Wharton, whose energy and passion are worthy of a prince's ransom.

Kyra Ryan provided in-depth suggestions and judicious editing in the formation of the manuscript. She has the mind of a poet and the heart of an artist, one who sees the warp and woof of a story. She has my deepest gratitude.

The late Liza Nelligan, a gifted editor and remarkable human being with whom I worked on a previous book, sadly passed away from cancer while I was writing this novel. At one point I had told her that I wanted to name a character after her and, being the self-conscious, humble person that she was, she insisted that I not do so while she was living. After that, she said, all bets were off. So, dear Liza, a woman of amazing strength who so inspired me, and so many others—the character of Liza Swain is for you.

I am indebted to Sue Booth-Forbes and the Anam Cara Writer's Retreat on the Beara Peninsula in West Cork, Ireland. Sue is spectacularly encouraging and she, assisted by the convivial Maureen O'Sullivan, buoyed me with good food, much humor, and the lilt of their spirit each day of my stay in Ireland.

Jon and Lili Bosse are precious friends whose continual support and belief in me go beyond friendship. The astoundingly gracious Jack Berman and Pearl Brown generously provided me with the use of their mountain home, where a portion of this book was written. As ever, thanks to dear friends for their ongoing support: Loren Judaken, Izzy and Rita Eichenstein, Karen and Ken Scopp, David and Jocelyn Lash, Mel Powell, Lori Bertheleson, Pat Ogden, and Dirk and Linda Wassner.

I so appreciate the constant support of my brothers and sister and their spouses: Michael and Cheryl Goldstein, Mark and Kyoko Goldstein, and Ethel Goldstein and John Eckerson. My brother-in-law, Glenn Solomon, a gifted lawyer, graciously provided me with background on a point of law that is integral to the novel. I thank him and his wife, Linda, for their encouragement.

My in-laws, Matt and Marion Solomon, unflaggingly share with me their precious insights, invaluable suggestions, and remarkable cheer.

My adult children have been astoundingly supportive of my creative endeavors since they were small: Yaffa, Batsheva, and Elisha, joined now by their respective spouses, Chris, Andy, and Stefanie (and by extension their little ones: Asher, Isabella, Chaz, Shai, Max, and Tali). With my marriage to Bonnie, I added Ari to that number, and two years later along came my now six-year-old, Shira. Individually and collectively, all my children transform and enrich my life.

What success I have as a person and as a writer I owe to my late father and mother, Frank and Roberta Goldstein, and their example of making a difference in the world and ever pursuing the artistic impulse.

And my deepest and most humble thanks to my wife, Bonnie. She is my first reader, an erudite critic when she needs to be, and always my most exuberant cheerleader. She has taught me a great deal about perseverance and love (and to be out in nature whenever possible, no matter the weather).

When you have someone in your life who believes in you like this, you can do anything.

The

PRINCE

of

NANTUCKET

1

Teddy Mathison shot out of the limo into a wild stampede of enthusiastic supporters and a mad crush of media. As he strode toward the battery of microphones outside the Walt Disney Concert Hall—Frank Gehry's dramatic architectural triumph, with its billowy silver curves—a cheer went up from a contingent of female groupies who'd begun appearing at his campaign events. The press had dubbed them "Teddy's Steadies."

This day, this crowd, and this building were the perfect backdrop for a candidate known for his out-of-the-box charisma. Security created a corridor for Teddy, who worked the crowds on either side, smiling broadly, keeping up an ongoing engaging banter while hastily signing objects and scraps of paper as they were thrust at him.

Observing the hoopla from the sidewalk, Judith Mackey, a forty-year-old powerhouse brunette, couldn't help but marvel. It had been like this at every stop since Teddy threw his hat into the race to become his party's candidate for the U.S. Senate. The savvy campaign manager who could have been the head of a movie studio but chose instead the even more cutthroat world of politics knew she had a winner the minute she signed on. Not only was Teddy a respected defense attorney, but he was also blessed with movie-star good looks and a knack for saying the right thing at the right time. On top of that, he possessed the "it" factor: Men wanted to be around him; women wanted to have his baby.

Even so, Judith knew only too well that under normal circumstances Teddy wouldn't be in this position. With the incumbent, Fitz Brady, felled by a sudden debilitating heart condition, it would normally fall to the party pols to handpick someone to run in the upcoming fall election. Several congressmen had been waiting years for the "promotion." Yet the free-spirited Senator Brady had surprised everyone by publicly calling for a special late-summer primary to allow the voters to decide for themselves who should run in his stead. While Teddy Mathison was a natural, Judith had harbored one fear about his candidacy.

And the latest polling results an aide had just handed her were confirmation that she'd been right.

2

His breath coming in spurts, Teddy made his way up Nob Hill surrounded by other runners and trailed by a host of photographers. He might have been relishing the attention, but his campaign manager was positively giddy. Having Teddy take part in the Women's Breast Cancer Network's 10K run in San Francisco had been Judith's idea. Sure, the candidate's good looks and aura of power were an aphrodisiac for some. But the hard-driven campaign manager knew that others were suspicious of Teddy. Events like the cancer run and the upcoming appearance before the Women's Political Caucus in San Diego were meant to show the empathic Teddy, in touch with women's issues and concerns.

"I can't believe you've had me doing phone interviews while running this race," Teddy huffed into his headset as he climbed the hill.

"Did I tire you out that much last night?" Judith quipped into her cell phone as she studied his beaming image on a monitor set up at the finish line.

"There you go," Teddy teased, tossing a thumbs-up at a camera, "making a joke of our 'recreational proclivities.' And, by the way, I'd appreciate it if we could just lie there for a few minutes afterward without having to talk about the latest polls."

The campaign manager glanced down at a report. "You boys have been doing it for thousands of years, right? Call me a convert. News cycles move fast. We have to move faster. Postcoital niceties are a luxury we can ill afford." She signed off on the report and held it out for an assistant.

"How about we *ill afford* those little precinct breakdowns you whisper in my ear while we're doing it," Teddy joked, flashing his trademark grin at a group of women screaming his name. "Is that some kind of aphrodisiac for you or do you just have to keep busy?"

"What can I say?" Judith shrugged. "I'm a *multitasker*. Now, good news or bad news?"

"Neither," Teddy grunted, smiling over at three attractive women holding one of his campaign signs. "I've got to focus on the crowd. I might spot my next great relationship."

"You and a relationship? Please," Judith said, looking first at the news crews then down at her watch. "You're not the type, Teddy. It's part of your perverse appeal with the ladies."

"I'm not buying that," Teddy said with a shake of his head. "I just need the *right* woman. The question is, does she exist?"

"God knows, there's no 'right' man," Judith mumbled, distracted by an e-mail she was sending. "Why should *She* have created a 'right' woman?"

"You think Rove mocked Bush this way when he was running his campaigns?" Teddy sighed.

"And then some," Judith teased, studying a message on her BlackBerry. "Relationships, Teddy, are for *other* people. Those willing to 'let go.' People who *settle*. You and I live by a different code. We're 'no-strings' people. We can't be bound." She glanced at a note handed to her by an aide, nodded, and handed it back. "That's what keeps us from making foolish commitments we have no intention of honoring." She paused. "Unless, of course, it wins votes. Then, what the hell?"

"A campaign manager who is sexy *and* devoid of principles," Teddy bantered. "How can I possibly lose?"

"One way," Judith said, sliding into her concern with the latest numbers. "Latest data shows you've got a fourteen-point lead over Emerson. Seventeen over Hoyt."

"Wow," he said, acknowledging well-wishers on the curb. "What could be bad?"

Judith turned around and gazed off at a father hoisting his kid on his shoulders for a better view of the finish. "Your family values numbers are coming in low. It's probably the divorce. People like to see their politicians married, for some perverse reason. The point is, you've got to let me—"

"No," he said, knowing full well what she was going to say.

"Teddy . . . ?"

"I said no."

"She's your daughter, for crying out loud," Judith pleaded. "Let the people see a few photographs of you playing the dutiful dad. Buying her ice cream. Biking together at the beach. Would it kill you? Women voters eat that right up."

A roar went up as Teddy passed a group holding a Mathison campaign banner. He pumped his fist. "We're not putting Zoe on parade to score some political points," he barked through his smile. "She's thirteen, Judith, and she's off-limits. Got it?"

Judith grimaced and shook her head. "You're making a mistake."

"Judith . . . ?" he spat, picking up the pace as he crested the hill.

"Yeah," she shot back brusquely, not used to losing. "I've got it."

"Good," he gasped as he raced toward the finish line. "Now find out who that cute blonde in the Stanford T-shirt is just ahead of me."

Judith caught sight of the stunning twentysomething completing her race.

"Forget it. You'd never keep up with her," she needled, flipping the phone shut.

Coming across the finish line, covered in sweat, enjoying applause and congratulations from the organizers, Teddy tossed his headset to an aide, posed for the cameras, and joked with onlookers. As he toweled off, he spotted the blonde a few yards away. She was boldly checking him out, her body glistening with the aftereffects of her run. Grinning, Teddy nodded in her direction, his breathing still ragged. He was about to make his way over to her when an aide ran up, a cell phone in his outstretched hand.

"It's for you," the young man said. "It sounded like it was kind of important."

Reluctantly, Teddy turned away from the blonde and did something he would immediately regret.

He took the call.

3

The strident voice of his older sister, Joanna, barreled at Teddy through the phone.

"The Alzheimer's has gotten worse. We're taking her to the island for the summer. You need to stop whatever you're doing and come see her now."

"Look, Jo, this really isn't a good time . . ."

"It's never a good time, is it, Teddy?"

Teddy waved at some of his supporters, flashing a thumbs-up for the cameras. "Jo, what do you want from me? I send you money, just like always. You get her what she needs."

"What she needs is for her only son to get his ass to Nantucket so he can spend some time with her before she's gone," Joanna said tartly. "Her hold on reality is slipping away, Teddy."

"I can't believe you expect me to do this, Joanna." Teddy turned and caught Judith's look of concern as she huddled with several aides twenty feet away. "You know better than anyone how I feel about her," he said quietly, signaling his campaign manager that there was nothing to worry about, though he knew that couldn't be further from the truth.

"I'm not asking, Teddy," his sister stated firmly. "We're way past requests."

Teddy gazed out at the beckoning waters of San Francisco Bay. "It's incredible what you've done for her, Jo," he said, as a young girl slipped into the cordoned-off area with paper and pen. "But look, we all make our choices . . ." He bent down and scribbled his name, patting the kid on the head, aware every minute of the position of the cameras.

"Right," Joanna snapped. "Some of us take care of those we love, while others move thousands of miles away so they don't have to."

"Jo," Teddy soothed, trying to placate her. "Be reasonable. I'm in the middle of a primary here. Your little brother might be the next senator from California. How about that?" he boasted. "Maybe you need to hire somebody full-time. The money is not a problem."

"What kind of world are you living in?" Joanna cut in. "I'm telling you our mother is losing her hold on reality. She's your mother, too, Teddy, like it or not. I'm not going to be grateful for the money and go away."

"Jo, listen to me . . . ," Teddy begged, feeling the battle going badly.

"No, you listen to *me*," Joanna shot back. "My marriage needs attention and I can't remember when I last had a break.

I am exhausted and she is in need. So you are going to come to Nantucket and be with her for the next two weeks or so help me, Teddy . . ."

"Come on, Jo," Teddy teased. "We're not kids anymore. What are you going to do to me, take away my ice cream like you used to?"

"No. I can do better than that," Joanna said, her voice steady and firm. "'Have you heard about the hotshot California senatorial candidate who can't be bothered to come to the bedside of his dying mother?' What's your guess, Teddy?" she taunted. "You think a reporter or two might be interested in *that* story?"

Teddy stood motionless, stunned. "Jo, I'm your brother, for God's sake!"

"You get to the island by the weekend, Teddy, or I will make calls to CNN, Fox News, and *USA Today.* It won't be pretty."

"Jo!"

"By the weekend or else," she warned. "For once in your life, Teddy, *show up.*"

4

Back in L.A., Teddy paced the beautiful stretch of sand known as the Malibu Colony, Judith trailing behind. It wasn't the expensive mix of modern and classical architecture lining this exclusive slice of beachfront that had drawn him here. Over the years, he found that this seashore had an almost magical appeal; it was here that he would plot out the final arguments he would make to a jury or ponder major decisions in his life. The quiet, the sand on his bare feet, and the glorious view of the ocean helped him think more clearly, something he was having trouble doing at the moment.

"You're not hearing me," Judith called out, zigzagging to avoid the surf. "Think of the angle: 'Candidate leaves the campaign trail to rush to the bedside of his dying mother.' I mean, hey, it's a pity she's sick, but are you *kidding*? This story and a few choice photos and your *family values* numbers shoot through the roof."

"You don't get it, Judith, do you? I just can't be around my mother. There's history there. That's all I'm going to say." He lowered the bill of his baseball cap and walked away.

His campaign manager chased after him, waving the heels she was carrying for emphasis. "Look. I get that your mother's not your favorite person. I'm not asking you to forgive her for whatever she did to you. But, hey, we don't all get a happy childhood."

Teddy stopped, fixing her with an icy glare, then turned his attention to the water.

"You've got a real shot at the Senate here, Teddy. You can't afford to have your sister going to the press. Way I see it, you fly in there, spend a little time, get a photo or two, and come right back. Sis is happy. The voters are impressed. Everybody wins."

Digging his hands deep into his pockets, Teddy scanned the waves moving toward him and imagined them carrying advice. "Talk to me," he whispered. A sinking feeling gripped him. He couldn't fathom setting foot on the island where, so many years ago, no thanks to one parent, he had lost the other.

"Here." Judith gestured, calling up the campaign date book on her BlackBerry. "You fly out day after tomorrow, Friday, that's June fourteenth, right? You stay a few days, a week, and you're back to campaign and then address the party movers and shakers on the twenty-eighth." She paused. "Strange. What's this 'Z' with a line through the next two weeks?"

"Christ, it's my daughter, Zoe. I get her full time only two weeks a year, always at the end of school. She'll be with me starting this weekend, Judith! This is not happening." He began walking again. "It's been three years since the divorce, but Zoe still treats me like I'm some criminal. It's brutal. I can't have her with me on that island when I face my mother, Judith. I'm telling you, I'll never survive!"

"What's the problem?" Judith asked, shrugging it off. "You just tell your ex you need to postpone."

"Oh, really?" Teddy said, painfully amused. "You haven't met Miranda, have you, Judith?" He exhaled sharply. "She's you. Only with principles." He stared back out at the ocean. "That and one helluva grudge."

Judith's eyes opened wide. "Whoa," she said, duly impressed.

5

U n-fucking-believable!"

Standing in the foyer of the spacious Brentwood home he'd ended up paying for twice—once when he'd purchased it as a newlywed, the second when he lost it as an asset in divorce proceedings—Teddy faced off with his ex-wife.

"Zoe's with you full time, what, two weeks a year and you can't even handle that?" Miranda sputtered. "How are you ever going to handle the needs of the entire state of California?!" She pushed her honey-blond hair behind her ears.

Teddy threw up his hands, pleading his cause. "My mother is dying, Miranda. What do you want from me?"

"Your mother?" She half-choked on the word. "You mean the mother I never even met in the twelve years we were married? *That* mother?"

Teddy stared at her for a moment, determined not to endure yet another lecture. "Whatever. Look"—he shook his head—"I didn't come here to fight. This is an emergency and I have to postpone with Zoe. We'll set something up after the primary. That's just the way it is."

As she stood defiantly before him, hands on slender hips, Teddy couldn't help noting that the Pilates workouts and yoga his alimony was helping to pay for were having an effect. Not only did she have more energy, if such a thing were possible, but her new physique gave rise to the unsettling notion that, if it came down to it, she probably could *take* him.

Miranda crossed the inlaid cedar floor until her face was inches from his. "Let me tell *you* the way it is, Teddy. Zoe's therapist says your daughter is at risk. She's moody and withdrawn, and, God knows, she doesn't much care for you and the way you handled yourself during the divorce.

"Now, I don't give a damn whether you win the primary or end up a trivia question on *Jeopardy!,* but I do care about our daughter. She isn't a line item on your agenda that can be postponed. You need to spend time together, and if you have this sudden need to fly off to Nantucket and do your duty to your mother then that means Zoe goes with you. And *that,* Teddy," she insisted, her gaze unwavering, "is the way it's going to be."

Teddy paced the floor, panicking. "Miranda, be reasonable. What the hell would I do with her on Nantucket?"

"Here's an idea. Introduce her to her mysterious grandmother," Miranda retorted with a half-laugh, then walked away.

Teddy's eyes darted up the circular stairway and then over at the wood-paneled living room, as if he might find a solution there. His mind was racing, but before he could formulate a single idea, Miranda was back in his face.

"You know, we were married twelve years, ten of which we shared with Zoe," she said, her voice lowered but no less uncompromising. "I may not like you a lot but this much I'll give you: Deep down, under all the ego and the ambition, I know that you love her." Miranda's eyes filled with sad conviction. "This is an important time for her. She is stepping into young womanhood and she needs a father she can count on. If you want to keep her in your life, Teddy, I suggest you don't screw this up. I doubt she'll give you another chance."

Teddy blinked, staring into Miranda's eyes. The idea of taking his troubled daughter on this mission back to hell was unthinkable. But the notion that his thirteen-year-old would want to cut him out of her life for good hit too close to home.

"Even if I agreed with you," he said, trying to wrap his mind around the proposal, "we both know she's not going to want to go to Nantucket with me—"

"You've got that right," Zoe practically shouted from the top of the stairs.

Teddy looked up to find his daughter peering down at him contemptuously. She wore her dirty-blond hair loose and wild. Her face was pale and her petite body was wrapped, as usual, in a bulky long-sleeved pullover and faded jeans.

"I'll leave you two to work this out," Miranda murmured, before disappearing into the kitchen.

Zoe scowled as she slumped down the stairs, her unkempt locks crowding the delicate features of her pretty face. "Just so you know," she tossed off flippantly, "Mom's going on a cruise. New boyfriend. Cute, but a total nerd. Anyway, that's the only reason she's insisting that I go with you. I'm inconvenient for both of you." She flung herself on the overstuffed sofa.

There was a slight twinge in Teddy at the mention of Miranda's new boyfriend but he kept his focus. "Your mother's concerned about you, Zoe," he ventured uncomfortably. "We both are—"

"Save it," his daughter cut him off. "You're just using the guilt card because it's the only one you can think of to play. Where the hell's Nantucket anyway? Not that I'm going with you," she muttered, flipping through a magazine, pausing to rip out a page and place it on her lap.

Teddy drew closer, peering over her shoulder. He could make out the photo of a menacing, tattooed rocker, rings sprouting from every orifice in his head. He recoiled. Was this what she was into? He thought back to the little girl he used to know. The toddler who would crawl up on his chest as he lay beside her on the floor and giggle at the surprise on his face. The five-year-old who liked to burst into a room, stick out her hand, and have her father spin her like the skating partners she had seen in a Disney ice show. But that was all in another life. Teddy no longer knew how to communicate with Zoe. So for the past three years he'd fallen back on the only strategic ploy he could come up with—he pandered.

"Trust me, Zoe. I don't want to go to Nantucket, either, but I have to," he leveled. "But it's our time to be together, right? Every year, first two weeks of summer vacation? So, here's what I'm going to do." He flashed a hardworking grin, stepping in front of her. "We get back from Nantucket, I'll get you and a friend front-row seats for that rock group you talk about, what's their name, TV on the Patio."

"TV on the *Radio,*" Zoe corrected, rolling her striking green eyes.

"Right," Teddy offered hopefully.

An incredulous little laugh escaped Zoe's lips. And then, in the cool voice of a young woman who'd seen too much for her age, she said, "You know, Dad, you really should get yourself a dog. They like it when you throw them a bone."

Teddy ran the back of his hand against his lips, his mind racing. There had to be something she wanted. He searched his brain for inspiration. And then it came to him. He was sure Miranda would have his head on a spike but desperate times . . .

"How about if I spring you from Lassiter?" he blurted.

Zoe sat up.

For the past two years his daughter had done nothing but protest the private school he and Miranda had chosen for her. Zoe was furious with both of them because unlike most issues during and after their marriage, they had decided to hang together on this one. His willingness to give her what she'd been asking for was a total collapse of any small measure of parental authority left to him. But maybe he could rescind it when they returned, just say he misspoke, save himself from having to deal with Miranda's anger. Right. He'd have to handle this carefully.

"Put it in writing," Zoe said, daring him.

Teddy nodded slowly, both horrified and impressed. He'd just been *outlawyered.* Swallowing hard, he took a pen from his suit pocket.

6

Shortly after takeoff, Teddy looked over at his wispy-haired daughter. She was already putting on headphones and plugging into the music of her iPod, cutting herself off from communication. He realized yet again that Zoe was a puzzle he hadn't a hope of figuring out. When they landed at Boston's Logan Airport four and a half hours later and transferred to Cape Air for the forty-five-minute flight over to Nantucket, his daughter refused to walk with him, choosing to follow behind at a distance. Yeah, right, this was definitely going to be a bonding experience, Teddy groaned to himself.

When the Cessna ten-passenger took to the air, Teddy gripped the edge of his seat, staring down at the Massachusetts coastline. He tolerated big planes, but flying in puddle jumpers was, in his opinion, like being hurtled through space in a tin can. He could sense his breakfast making its way in the wrong direction. As the tiny plane bounced along, buffeted by winds, a portly woman seated next to him chose that moment to become chummy.

"Vacationing?" she yelled above the roar of the engine.

Teddy shook his head. "Visiting my mother," he replied, his body suddenly pressed into hers by a jarring updraft.

"Such a good son," she bellowed in his ear.

Teddy turned and stared out the window, tightening his grip on the seat cushion. No one had accused him of being a good son in many years. He glanced up to see how Zoe was faring, catching sight of the back of her head tucked into her sweater. It seemed to Teddy that she had withdrawn into a tiny cocoon and he wished he could crawl in there with her.

Before he knew it, Cape Cod was stretching out below him. The crescentlike peninsula marked the edge of America's mainland. Thirty miles farther out to sea and he spotted Nantucket, a boomerang-shaped spit of sand and windswept moors. Teddy realized with a start that he had never seen it from the air. As a child he always took the ferry to the island for summer breaks with his family. He used to thrill at the first sight of Nantucket from the boat, its church spires and flashing lighthouses, the great harbor reaching out like a pair of welcoming arms. A sudden dip in the plane lifted Teddy up against his seat belt, causing his seat partner to gasp and grab hold of his arm. Teddy's hand slammed up against the low ceiling to steady himself.

Peering out the window as the Cessna dipped yet again, Teddy scanned the magical island of his youth. Nantucket had been a safe haven for him as a boy, a place that also beckoned with adventure. As the plane descended, Teddy saw miles of sandy beaches and the quaint weathered gray houses that, even from the air, gave Nantucket a unique character. He could make out the island's westernmost tip in Madaket, home to glorious sunsets, and the vast moors where he once had romped in games of hide-and-seek in heather, scrub, and bogs of cranberries. And finally, at the easternmost edge of the island, he glimpsed Sconset, where the summerhouse was.

The island was rushing up to meet him, and a knot began twisting in his stomach; the bracing reality of his return was washing over him. For years he had willed himself not to think of this place, and now the island loomed through his window like a friend he no longer trusted.

He looked up to find Zoe again. She had no idea what this place meant to him because he'd never wanted to speak of it. Teddy thought of his ex-wife's words—"If you want to keep her in your life, Teddy, I suggest you don't screw this up. I doubt she'll give you another chance." Could it be his daughter would one day view him with the same revulsion he felt toward his mother? Teddy shuddered at the thought, then closed his eyes and held on as the wheels of the Cessna smacked the tarmac.

Staring out the window as they taxied, he saw a lone seagull taking flight off the roof of the modest newly shingled terminal. And then the plane was stopping.

What he wouldn't have given to have had wings.

7

Teddy-boy, over here!" It was a voice imprinted with a soft Irish lilt.

On the other side of the chain-link divider stood a red-faced, husky old gentleman Teddy hadn't laid eyes on since his last trip to the island shortly after law school. Frank Lafferty was nearly eighty now but Teddy would have known him anywhere.

"When I heard you were coming I got out my winter coat. I figured hell must have frozen over," Frank teased. "Well, let's have a look at you . . ."

Teddy was surprised to feel so awkward. He'd long ago allowed the part of his life that included Frank to fade from memory. Now, facing the man who'd once been like a second father to him, Teddy experienced a flash of guilt. The muscles in his neck tightened.

"So this is what a politician looks like." Frank grinned broadly.

Teddy looked taken aback.

"Oh, yes, we get the news out here. I follow what you're up to." The older man gave Teddy a firm handshake and then clapped him on the back in a quick hug. "It's good to see you, lad. It'll mean a lot to your mother."

Teddy let out a deep breath. "Yeah," he muttered, turning back to find Zoe sauntering through the gate alongside a pretty woman and her giggling toddler and an animated elderly couple dressed in his and her sailing outfits. What a gloomy contrast she was to them. He noted the uncomfortable look on her face as she scanned her surroundings warily. "Zoe, I'd like you to meet an old family friend, Frank Lafferty."

Frank eyed the girl's torn jeans and the frown that had taken over her face. He took a step toward her, tufts of his white hair blowing in the summer breeze. "He's got the 'old' right, I'll give him that." Frank laughed. "Welcome to Nantucket, Zoe."

She fidgeted with the straps of her backpack. "Thanks," she mumbled, before glancing up without emotion and gesturing toward her father. "He doesn't want to be here, you know."

"Zoe!" Teddy shot back.

"Hey"—she shrugged nonchalantly—"neither do I." Taking out her iPod, she put her headphones back on, tuning them out.

"Well then," said Frank, exhaling cautiously, "we'll just see about those bags."

Teddy turned and eyed him. Frank's gait was stiff and he seemed to favor his left side ever so slightly as he headed toward the baggage area. Teddy could recall the power that had once filled the Irishman's body, his muscles developed from working outdoors, carrying lumber, fixing houses, not to mention maneuvering his beloved sailboat in and out of the water. There was strength yet in the old physique but it had been sorely weathered over the years. Taking a deep breath, Teddy wondered what changes he might find in his mother.

Twenty minutes later, after they'd retrieved their luggage and left the terminal, Teddy sat in the front of Frank's beat-up station wagon, his sullen daughter in the rear seat behind him. Frank held his tongue. Teddy's breathing was shallow. Staring out the window at the host of evergreens lining the road, he felt like a condemned man on his way to the gallows.

The older man drove them down a winding narrow road. They passed acres of vast open space, tall grass, and an occasional pond on either side.

"You remember how we used to hike the moors, Teddy? You could name every one of those flowers by the time I got done with you," Frank said, trying to break the palpable tension in the car.

Teddy fidgeted in his seat and checked his cell. A number of messages had piled up, all from Judith. He punched in the number but the reception was poor and it was hard to hear through the static.

"Those things don't always work so well out here," the Irishman said, eyeing Teddy's cell. "You'll get a stronger signal in town and out in Sconset. I don't know what everyone has to say that's so all important it can't wait until they get home," he said, shaking his head.

As the magnificent view of the ocean came into sight, Frank called back to Zoe. When she didn't answer, Teddy immediately turned and flashed her a look.

"What?" she responded, reluctantly removing her head-phones.

Frank piped up. "There you are. Just thought you'd be inter-ested to know that your father learned to surf in these waters. Wasn't too bad at it, as I remember."

Zoe had never seen her father surf and Teddy remained silent, certain his daughter was puzzling her way through the incongruous image of her father "hanging ten." And then, turn-ing to his left, he caught sight of the lighthouse. Immediately, his heart started beating faster. They were almost there.

"Sankaty Head," Frank announced, pointing to his left.

Teddy's anxiety increased as Frank eased the car down a street filled with homes of all sizes, each covered in Nantucket's distinc-tive weathered gray shingles. Despite his nerves, Teddy couldn't help noticing the changes that had taken place since last he'd been there. New upscale residences had replaced many of the unas-suming saltboxes that had once marked the neighborhood.

Frank pulled the car into a small driveway in front of the last and only untouched edifice on the street. The drab shingles looked as if they'd been through the worst of weather. The white paint on the front railing was peeling back and whole patches on the roof trim had fallen away, leaving the wood beneath exposed.

Teddy sat in the car staring at the familiar two-story house. His eyes traced their way across the weathered gray facade. He felt numb. Looking up, he found Frank already had the bags on the front porch and was gazing intently back at him. Teddy knew that look from his childhood. Whenever he'd been unsure he could do something—sail a boat, bike across island and back, own up to his parents about something he'd done wrong—Frank had fixed him with the same expression, which seemed to say, *You can do this, boy. So let's get on with it, now.*

Taking a deep breath, Teddy rubbed his face vigorously and got out of the car. Reluctantly putting one foot in front of the other, he headed up the well-worn steps.

8

Just inside the entrance, Teddy stopped to get his bearings. The two-story house was as he remembered it: narrow hallway, worn wooden banister leading upstairs, walls chock-full of framed sketches and brightly colored beach scenes of all shapes and sizes. Zoe was already moving down the cramped foyer into the large sitting room with its oversize stuffed chairs, a wraparound russet sofa that had seen better days, and large sunny windows with sheer lace curtains. Wandering in behind her, Teddy was struck by the sight of his daughter in the summer home of his youth. Two worlds colliding. He observed the way she poked around, sizing up the place, recognizing himself in her idle curiosity. At her age he'd never waited to be shown around. He'd felt the only opinion that could be trusted was his own.

"Teddy, Zoe," Frank interrupted, accompanied now by a short middle-aged woman, "meet Annie Forbes. Finest nurse on the island."

"I'm no kind of a nurse. Just a caretaker," corrected the

stout, fiftyish lady, drying her hands on her apron. She seemed instantly taken, as so many were, with the handsome and powerful Teddy Mathison. As if drawn to a magnet, she went directly to him and her words tumbled out like water from a teapot boiling over. "Your mother's in the studio. She prefers it there. We've told her you're coming, but I'm not sure she remembers. She drifts. Well, you'll see for yourself." She paused, growing flushed. "I've read about you in the papers, Mr. Mathison." She giggled nervously.

"Well, how industrious of you, Annie," Frank said tartly. "And I'm sure you have a million things to do," he added, shooing her along while turning to Zoe. "Young lady, what's say we give your father and grandmother a chance to get reacquainted while I show you to your room." The Irishman winked, steering the moody teen out of the room and up the stairs before she could launch a protest.

Teddy held his breath. Glancing over at the paintings hanging on the walls around him, he could remember when they were blank canvases. His mother was nothing less than a magician to him back then, a wondrous alchemist with the marvelous secret for transforming simple oils into priceless art. That, of course, was before the magic died and he had come to see her for what she truly was.

Teddy let out his breath all at once then bit hard on his lip, drawing blood. "Let's get it over with," he muttered, and headed out to see what awaited him in the back studio.

9

Ducking his head under the low doorway, Teddy entered the room and paused, temporarily blinded. The studio was bathed in the brilliance of the sunset. Golden rays of light poured in through a large glass window that framed the ocean. Teddy strained his eyes in the slanted light that suffused the room. And then he saw her. There, in the only dark pocket of the studio, under the shadow of a large piece of driftwood nailed to the wall, sat the still figure of his mother.

Teddy squinted, trying to make out whether the older woman was staring into space or simply waiting him out. He found himself glancing over at the doorway, hoping Frank or Zoe would come in and save him. Taking a couple of tentative steps in his mother's direction, Teddy was relieved to find her sleeping. Emboldened, he ventured closer, hunching down a few feet from her to get a better look.

Her white hair was done up in a soft yellow bow that pulled it back off her face. Her skin looked paper-thin, almost translucent.

Years ago, when she held sway on Nantucket and within the art circles of Boston, she had been considered "a patrician beauty," a moniker that hadn't sat well with Teddy's fiercely independent mother. "Patrician" was a word better suited for the queen of England, she told him, not an artist.

As he gazed into her once-beautiful face for the first time in years, the reality of her ruin sent an odd ache coursing through him. The anger he was used to, but this dull pain threw him. He wanted it to go away, and he shook his head as if he could make it do so.

Rising, Teddy looked around the room. It was mostly as he remembered: brushes tidy in glass jars, palettes stacked on a shelf, oils along the windowsills, blocks of watercolors sitting in a custom-made rack Frank had fashioned years ago. There were blank canvases of various sizes stacked against the floorboards and two works, one a sketch, the other a partial composition, mounted on easels by the large center window. His eyes came to rest on the unfinished painting. Like many of his mother's works, it was of the ocean. She had always favored alternating her medium, painting some works in watercolors and others in oils. For this one she had chosen particularly vibrant oils. He glanced back to assure himself that she was still sleeping, then turned to study the composition.

Teddy stared at the uncompleted painting, and it came to life before his eyes. The waves rose magnificently and a line of seagulls skimmed the surface of the water, searching for food. Out in the ocean, figures in a boat appeared to be kissing. The glow of a setting sun infused the work. The same golden light that now flooded the studio had been transported onto the canvas. As he continued to stare intently at the painting, the water, astonishingly, appeared to be moving.

Teddy caught his breath and stepped closer. His mother was an accomplished artist to be sure, but what he was looking at had a unique quality he'd never seen in her work. And yet the bottom third of the painting, where the beach might be, along with a prominent swatch in the upper right-hand corner, were all empty, untouched. It was as if she had discovered a whole new method of mixing and applying paint and then, midway through her masterpiece, lost the gift along with her mind.

Teddy turned and, curious, sat down opposite her. Joanna had said their mother was "disappearing," but his sister had always possessed a flair for drama, and he hadn't really paid much attention. It was his opinion that Joanna had made a habit of crying wolf over the years in a misguided attempt to pull their family back together. But he would have none of it. There was not a lot in life that Teddy found constant and absolute. Witnesses could be torn down, facts finessed to fit one's argument. Yet the evidence in the case of his mother was not circumstantial or malleable in any way. It was the foundation upon which Teddy had staked his career. *People lie, betray, obfuscate.* They destroy those they love. His mother was de facto evidence for this finding. She'd been judged and convicted by his jury of one, long ago.

Now, as Teddy took in the striking decline of her physical appearance, the possibility that Joanna had been telling the truth unnerved him. His mother appeared used up, like one of her paint tubes squeezed dry. The woman he had long pushed away from the boundaries of his life was now unmasked and unthreatening. He wanted to remind her that she had wrecked his life because she cared more for her art than she did for his father. Suddenly, he felt like screaming. She had broken up their home, destroyed their family, driven his father to the edge of his senses, and shattered Teddy's dreams.

Leaning in, Teddy studied the woman he had scorned for so many years, a mother he'd once loved so much he would have died for her.

"My God," he whispered in utter amazement. "Look at what's become of the great Kate Longley Mathison."

10

The old woman stirred, slowly awakened, and looked at him. There was a quizzical look on her face and she closed and opened her eyes several times like the lens of a camera being brought into focus.

"It's me, Mom, Teddy," he whispered, his voice gentle and boyish. There was a quivering within him that he was having trouble controlling. For all his anger, it was pitiful to see a force of nature reduced to this.

"I've got Zoe with me. Your granddaughter? I never wanted her to know you at all and now *this* is how she'll meet you," he lamented, his voice catching in his throat.

A light flickered in her irises before steadying. Kate appeared to transform before his eyes. Then, out of her mouth came the unmistakable cadence of a Boston Brahmin.

"Well, well," Kate said. "Look who's finally come home."

Taken aback, Teddy stared into the weathered yet alert face of his mother. "You—you know me? I—I thought . . ."

"Of course I know you." Kate tsked. "Goodness. You don't show your face for years and all you can do is stutter? Pull yourself together and stand in front of me. Let me get a good look at you."

Off balance, Teddy found himself obeying. Standing there, letting her look him over, he felt awkward, like a child. It appeared that despite the loss of her once natural beauty, his mother was alive and well and as forceful as ever.

"You're older," she noted bluntly. "Well, it can't be helped. Look at me," she said, shaking her head. "The gods have not been kind, wouldn't you agree?"

"Well, actually . . . ," Teddy began.

"Don't say anything. That's a rhetorical question."

Teddy eyed his mother suspiciously. Where was the Alzheimer's Joanna carried on about? This woman seemed as sharp as a tack and as utterly dismissive as ever.

"You have a lot of explaining to do but we'll leave that for now," Kate declared, trying to get up but letting out a groan of pain instead. "My body is rebelling. It won't listen to me."

Shaking his head, Teddy marveled that nothing had changed in his absence. Seventeen years had gone by since he'd graduated from Harvard and left the East Coast. In that time he'd been back exactly once, to pick up some of his personal belongings and try a rapprochement at Joanna's urging.

"But the biggest betrayal, the one I cannot forgive, is my hands. They just don't work, Teddy. My mind can't seem to make them. Now *that* is intolerable." Kate stuck out her arm. "Well?" she barked, her eyes on her son. "Are you going to help me or stand there staring like some lost schoolboy?"

Teddy winced. It was comments like that one that had once driven him crazy. It wasn't the reason he had walked out of her life, but her brusqueness had made it easier. He stepped forward grudgingly and helped her to her feet. Her skin felt like crepe paper and his own body recoiled at the touch of her. Then, suddenly, he felt his mother shudder as she sunk into him.

"Hello," came the small voice in the doorway.

Steadying his mother, Teddy looked up to find Zoe standing there, staring intently as if at a ghost.

"Who is this?" Kate demanded as if finding an intruder in her home.

"This is my daughter," Teddy said tersely. "Zoe, this is your grandmother, Kate."

Zoe examined the strange figure before her—the distant look, the fragile, wrinkled skin, the loose ends of white hair. Who was this woman to her, anyway? Zoe had no memory of her. She took a few tentative steps closer.

"Hello?" Zoe ventured nervously.

"Zoe . . . ," Teddy cautioned.

"Should I call you Grandma? I call my other grandmother Grammie."

The older woman stared back at her sternly. "Here now," she said, looking her over, eyes flashing impatiently. "What is it you do?"

"What do I do . . . ?" Zoe repeated.

Teddy saw how his mother was staring at Zoe. He knew that look, the one that saw right through you. He wanted to move to his daughter and shield her from it but he was stuck there, holding the old woman up. He watched anxiously as a curious Zoe drew closer, studying her grandmother's face.

"What are you looking at?" Kate asked irritably.

"Katie," Frank cautioned, appearing in the doorway. "Easy now. This is your granddaughter, Zoe."

"My grand . . . ?" Kate blinked. It didn't register.

Zoe came toward her, opening her arms.

"What is this?" the older woman snapped, withdrawing. "Don't put your hands on me."

"My other grandmother always wants a hug," Zoe stammered. "I just thought . . ."

"No," Kate objected.

"That's it, Mother," Teddy barked as he managed to park her down on the chair. "I won't have you behaving that way to my daughter."

Something in the older woman seemed to deflate. Kate suddenly appeared lost. "Who?" She gazed up at Zoe, then at her son, frightened. "You're my . . . I'm—" She broke off, her voice faltering.

"What's going on?" Teddy demanded, turning to Frank. "What just happened?"

"It's the Alzheimer's," Frank sadly explained as he crossed the studio, pulling an afghan over Kate. "She goes in and out like the tide."

Zoe stared at the strange woman she was supposed to be related to. This "grandmother" had just rejected her and then weirdly morphed into some kind of lost child. Hurt and confused, she turned on her father. "Why did you have to bring me here?" she blurted, then ran from the room.

Teddy watched her go, his body coursing with emotion. His icy heart had cracked at the sight of his mother in ruin. He wanted to reach out to his troubled daughter but was responsible for triggering an even greater abyss, managing to disappoint her once again.

Turning back, Teddy gazed at the helpless, tentative figure who had been his mother but a moment ago. It was like something out of *Dr. Jekyll and Mr. Hyde.* He had the sudden urge to contact his campaign staff, answer a few e-mails, anything to take his head out of this place.

"It's the light that makes them dance," Kate suddenly called out as she stared at her unfinished painting. Teddy shook his head. What was she talking about?

"It's the light . . . it makes them . . ." Her voice faltered and faded away.

Who had pulled the plug on this woman's mind? My God, she didn't need him there, he told himself. What was he supposed to do for her, anyway? Still, observing her retreat into herself held him spellbound, like coming upon an accident and being repelled but unable to turn away.

A sudden memory pried loose from its vault. It was after the first art lesson she'd given him. He was six, maybe seven. He'd become so frustrated at not being able to make his brush do what he wanted that he had stuck his hand in the paint and placed its imprint smack in the middle of the canvas, declaring,

"Me!" He had waited, expecting his mother's disapproval. Instead, she burst into a cheer and swooped him up in her arms. "You," she acknowledged, swinging him so hard he thought he'd fly right through the window. Her response had scared and thrilled him and made him feel suddenly important.

Pushing the memory away, Teddy cursed his sister for forcing this trip on him and, turning, strode from the studio.

11

Teddy shot up in bed, drenched in sweat, a bad dream lapping at the edges of his consciousness.

Rubbing his forehead, he checked the time—five A.M. He caught his breath, then reached automatically for his cell to retrieve messages. But the signal inside the house was too weak. He had to get a paper, turn on the news, find out what was happening back in California. He got up and checked on Zoe down the hall. Gently pushing the door open, he was relieved to find her under the covers. It had taken him an hour and a phone call to Miranda to calm her down after her encounter with her grandmother. He had promised both of them he would find something fun for Zoe to do *away* from the house for the few days they would be there.

A jarring clatter caught his attention. He closed Zoe's door and listened as the nagging rattle persisted, punctuated by a few seconds of silence before it struck again. Irritated, Teddy made his way down the hall. The sound appeared to be coming from his mother's bedroom. The door was ajar. He thought about retreating but the noise was only growing louder. Shaking his head, Teddy gritted his teeth and pushed the door open farther.

Peering in, Teddy made out Kate's face illuminated by the small night-light next to the bed. She was still asleep. How could she manage with the din going on in her room? The rattling struck again and Teddy crossed over to the window for inspection. He could see now that the shutter on the left had broken off from the side of the house and was banging away in the wind coming off the ocean. Teddy awkwardly removed the screen and reached out, grabbing hold of the errant shutter. As he grappled with it in an attempt to hook it back into place, it tore from its sole mooring and fell away from his hand to the ground below.

"Damn place is falling apart," he muttered, staring down at the shutter, which had broken into pieces upon impact. Jerking his head back, he bumped it hard on the window frame. A sharp pain shot through him.

"Shit!" he cried out.

"Who is it? Who's there?" demanded a startled voice.

Rubbing the back of his head, Teddy twisted around to face his mother, who was now sitting up in bed.

"You had a broken shutter," he muttered. "I was trying to fix it. It's all right. Go back to bed." He picked himself up, nearly tripping over the window screen he'd put on the floor moments earlier.

"I don't need anyone making a racket like that in the middle of the night," Kate snapped.

Teddy held his tongue as the long-buried animosity flooded his brain. This was the same way she'd treated his father. No wonder the man stayed away for weeks at a time. Or that he turned to alcohol to escape her harangues. Teddy wanted to make his own escape. If he left now, Joanna couldn't possibly go to the press. He had proof he'd been there to visit. His mind raced. Get out, it said. You don't need this, it pleaded. He turned to leave.

"I'm not sure," came a frail voice he didn't recognize. "Did you just help me?"

Teddy held his breath.

"I'm sorry I can't . . . ," she struggled. "Did you just . . . ?"

"Yes, Mother," Teddy finally answered, not looking back at her.

"I thought so." She sighed, tremulous. "That was sweet of you. You're a good boy."

Head reeling, Teddy thought he'd keel over. He couldn't remember the last time she'd spoken to him like that, so soft and caring. It had to have been before his father's death, of that he was sure. It was as if someone else had suddenly taken possession of her body. As if a hidden force were changing channels in her head. Could the Alzheimer's really be doing that? Could it really tame the devil in a person?

As much as he wanted to leave the room, Teddy couldn't help turning around to look at his mother. She was illuminated by the moonlight. Her head was resting on the pillow; she lay there, still. It was unsettling to find her smiling at him. Her face showed no vestiges of disease, just the lines and wrinkles of life's road map. Teddy couldn't take his eyes off her. She was suddenly gentle-looking, beautiful in her own way, the sting drawn out of her.

As he continued to glance down at the bed, fixated, another memory jumped out at him. He was five, Joanna seven. With his dad back in the city during the midweek summer days, Kate would allow them a once-a-week pajama night. They'd eat popcorn and she would tell them stories about magical sea creatures and kingdoms of incredible beauty under the ocean's surface. What had happened to that woman? He felt breathless. The sudden recollection was painful, disconcerting, and totally unexpected.

His mother's eyes were now gazing up at the ceiling and he detected they were out of focus. She appeared to be lost in her own bed. The sight of her like this was nearly unbearable. She remained, after all these years, a mystery to him. More unwanted memories were jarring loose within him, and he angrily fought to push them away. Teddy turned and quickly retreated from the room.

Racing up the stairs to the attic, Teddy threw open the roof door and walked out onto the rail-enclosed lookout. Many homes in Nantucket had these modest roofwalks, or "widow's walks." The wives of the whaler captains, once the aristocracy of what was then the world's greatest whaling port, had spent endless evenings staring out to sea, wondering if their men would ever come home. Teddy clasped the railings as he had when he was young. He closed his eyes and took in the salty smell, a breeze coming off the ocean whipping at his hair.

When the first light of dawn emerged out of the east, Teddy gazed up at the fog hanging overhead. It had been Frank who'd told him how sailors passing the island a hundred years earlier and noting the persistent haze had dubbed Nantucket "the Gray Lady."

His heart was still pounding from the second encounter with his mother as he turned northward, scanning the vast natural reserve that made up so much of the island. He could make out the gentle waters of Sesachacha Pond, separated from the ocean by a narrow strand on its east side. Beyond that stretched the shingled roofs of beach houses that made up the tiny hamlet of Quidnet.

Teddy noticed that the blanket of fog was moving. As he followed its billowing progress, it struck him that the gray mass was like his mother's mind. She, like the island, was disentangling from the world. He smiled grimly at the thought that his mother, the possessor and wielder of color, was becoming the Gray Lady. He had a guilty suspicion that had the Alzheimer's struck earlier he might have been able to stand her all these years.

Teddy turned to the east where the sun poked its head through the fog. He thought of the campaign going on without him on the other coast. Judith was no doubt spinning his absence as a mark of his deep concern for family. Inside the house were two women to whom he was related and yet both were strangers to him. Teddy rested his head in his hands. *What family?*

12

Later that morning, Teddy offered Annie twice her daily rate to come in on a Saturday and tend to Kate. Phoning Hertz, he arranged for the delivery of a jazzy, powder blue Infiniti convertible. Zoe might still be acting cool toward him but she had a hard time masking her approval at the first sight of the hot wheels. Besides, she wanted out of that house and away from her strange grandmother as much as he did.

Pulling into town, Teddy was struck by the bumper-to-bumper traffic on the cobblestoned Main Street. Flush with tourists, day-trippers, and SUVs ferried over, it was like being back in L.A. Somehow in his many years of absence the island had morphed into the Hamptons, *the* place to *do* summer. Spying a small opening between a Hummer and a Range Rover, Teddy managed to wedge in the convertible.

At a table in the courtyard of the Even Keel Cafe, a waitress, her auburn hair gathered into a ponytail, came by to take their order.

"Morning. I'm Liza," she greeted them. "What can I get for you?"

"A new life," Zoe tossed off, burying her head in the menu.

The waitress glanced over at Teddy, who tried not to look pained.

"I'll take scrambled eggs, a blueberry muffin, and a Coke," Zoe said, leaning back haphazardly in her chair.

"A Coke for breakfast?" Teddy repeated with mild surprise. "You sure?"

"Yup," replied Zoe, looking off, distracted.

"Because you know most people don't hit the hard stuff until at least noon."

Zoe shook her head. "Don't mind my father," she told the waitress. "This is him trying to relate."

Liza grinned in empathy.

Teddy smiled back, taking note of the attractive ringlets that framed the woman's face. He caught Zoe giving him the eye and turned back to the menu. "I'll have French toast, please. It says here the syrup is real Vermont maple?"

"Yes," Liza indicated. "Why, are you from Vermont?"

"Los Angeles," Teddy said and noted the nonresponse on her face. "I can see what you're thinking—everything's fake in L.A., right? What do they know about authenticity? Town of tinseled dreams where women buy their body parts direct from the plastic surgeon, but let me tell you," he insisted with a nod and a wink, "some of us out there still appreciate the real thing."

Liza arched an eyebrow. "I'll just go put your order in."

Zoe slid deep into her chair with a groan.

"What?" Teddy asked.

Zoe rolled her eyes. "You were like totally *coming on* to her."

"I was not," Teddy dismissed with a laugh.

"Right." Zoe shrugged. "You know, if you understood females even the tiniest bit you'd get that you're being an asshole." She crossed her arms, kicked her legs up onto a vacant chair, and disappeared into her iPod.

As far as Teddy was concerned, there were few people who had anything to teach him about talking to women. He knew what they liked, when they liked hearing it, and how to say it. But as he studied Zoe slumped in her chair, tethered to a digital sound track that tuned him out, he realized he had no idea what to say to *her*.

He took a good hard look at his daughter. For the first time he noticed her hair and how long it had become. A platinum streak her mother had let her put in months earlier had nearly grown out. Teddy observed the tiny freckles along the bridge of her nose, thinking back to how he used to kiss each one when she was a toddler and they first appeared. He took note now of her surprisingly graceful elongated fingers. In fact, she had grown long of limb all over in the last year. Then Teddy's eyes fell on . . . he froze. Where in the hell had *they* come from? Not pronounced yet, all right, especially in her baggy sweater, but definite signs of development. He quickly glanced away, not wanting Zoe to catch him staring at that part of her anatomy. How many women had he given the once-over to? he asked himself. And never once had he thought of them as somebody's daughter.

A young waiter arrived with their breakfasts and Zoe unplugged herself from the iPod and dived in. Teddy found it curious that even in the warm, sunny conditions, Zoe was still wearing heavy clothes with long sleeves. He guessed it had something to do with the way teenage girls were supposed to be uncomfortable with their bodies. If she had thoughts about that, what would it hurt to listen?

"Okay. Okay," he said, pulling closer, eager now to talk. "I'm in. So how should I talk to women?"

Suspicious, Zoe glanced up from her eggs. "What are you doing?"

"I'm saying, maybe I have something to learn. So what have you got?"

Zoe thought about it as she eyed him. "Okay," she agreed grudgingly. "These are the rules. One. You never flirt with a woman who is taking your order."

"What? Women love a little harmless . . ."

Zoe shot him a look.

Teddy shook his head. "Right. Flirting with waitresses is off the list. Next?"

"No jokes about the female anatomy," Zoe stated flatly.

Teddy lifted his eyebrows but nodded.

"Rule number three," Zoe said, leaning closer for effect. "Nothing happens in front of your teenage daughter . . . *ever!*" she commanded.

He stared back, wondering how many times he'd broken that one.

Glancing up, Teddy caught sight of the waitress leaning just close enough to listen in as she bused a nearby table. She immediately grew flushed and hurried off, clanking her bucket of glasses and dishes. Teddy turned back to Zoe as she slurped the end of her Coke. "All right. Good. Good. That was good," he pronounced. "You see, you and I can talk. We can do this." Teddy studied her. "We get back to California, what do you say you come out on the campaign trail with me, give me some pointers. Would you like that?"

Zoe stared up at him as if she might puke.

"I just thought, if we shared something like that, we could—"

"What?" Zoe cut him off. "Bond or something?" she said, letting loose a dismissive little laugh. "Have some daddy-daughter moments?" she taunted.

"Yeah." He searched her eyes. "I want to talk to you."

"Talk to me? About what?" she ridiculed.

"Things," Teddy exclaimed. "I don't know—school . . . boys . . ."

"Give me a break." Zoe laughed.

". . . the clothes you wear."

Zoe's smirk vanished. She stiffened. "What's wrong with my clothes?" she demanded.

"I don't know." Teddy shrugged, shaking his head. "Look at these other girls here," he said, gesturing at another teen in a cute blouse and shorts. "It's summer. Why not dress more like her?"

Zoe stood up, knocking over her chair in the process. It landed hard on its side and the restaurant went silent for a moment. She glanced around. The girl in the cute blouse was staring at her—everyone was. Flustered, Zoe rubbed her left arm nervously and flashed a look back at her father.

"Look, I'm not her, I'm me," she hissed with defiance. "I like what *I* like, all right? So get off my case!" With that, she ripped across the courtyard and out onto the street.

Teddy looked up to see Liza standing nearby.

"Sorry," he muttered, embarrassed. "We're done. I'll just put this on the table." He threw down a couple of twenties and ran out.

Teddy found his daughter waiting by the car, brooding. "I want to go home," she spat. "*My* home."

"You aren't the only one," Teddy said, unsettled.

As he drove back with her he couldn't help thinking that he knew how to lose a mother. He'd been doing it most of his life. But where do you learn how *not* to lose a daughter?

13

After kicking around the house for the rest of the day, trying to stay out of contact with anyone, Zoe lay on her bed deep into the night staring up at the ceiling. Several cracks intersected one another, paint flaking away from the surface and threatening to break away. She wanted to do the same. Her father had dragged her out here and so far it was a bust. Why wasn't she surprised? As for her mother, she was off having some hot time with the new boyfriend. What did Miranda care about anything Zoe was going through? On top of it, she still smarted from the way she'd been treated by the grandmother she'd just met. The woman seemed cruel, sickness or not. As pissed as she was at her father, it occurred to her that it couldn't have been any picnic growing up with Kate Mathison for a mother. In that moment, she almost felt sorry for him. Feeling confined, Zoe opened the door and stole out into the hallway.

She glanced around at the brightly painted, narrow corridor. She'd been so upset at being around her father and in this strange place that she hadn't really noticed it until now. Unlike down-stairs, the walls here were lined with photos. Zoe examined a few. Amid sepia-toned portraits from earlier eras, she found a picture that featured a woman with a little girl sitting on her lap. Her aunt Joanna had long brown hair and a tiny, turned-up nose that made her appear younger than she actually was. Zoe stared at the little girl and recognized herself. The photograph had been taken in their living room in California when her dad's sister had visited years ago. And yet, staring at herself as a three-year-old, Zoe couldn't recall ever being that small. It struck her that her grandmother must have wanted this photograph of her on the wall. She wondered if there were others.

Looking higher on the wall, Zoe found one that drew her interest immediately. Reaching up, she pulled it off its hook for closer inspection. Zoe knew she was seeing her father as a boy. Probably nine, maybe ten, she thought. He was in a baggy pair of bathing trunks, his face beaming as he stood knee-deep in the water. His arms were locked in a powerful hug around the neck of a beautiful, robust woman Zoe recognized to be a younger version of her grandmother. She studied her father's face, the big-tooth grin, the mischief in his eyes. It was so uncalculated. He wasn't playing to a jury or to voters or to a daughter. It was odd to see him unmasked and happy.

She came upon framed magazine covers and paused. Here was her grandmother on the covers of *Time* and *Newsweek*. One bore the caption "The Modern Master Is a Woman" and featured a much younger Kate painting in her studio. The other declared, "Kate Longley Mathison: Artist of the Decade."

Zoe gazed at the covers. Her grandmother had been a major big deal.

Zoe heard coughing. She didn't move. There was a pause and then a weak voice called out.

"Could you turn my bedside light off, dear?"

Zoe's breath caught in her throat. Pivoting around, she saw now that she was standing opposite her grandmother's bedroom. The door was slightly ajar, a small glow coming from within. How had the older woman known she was there? Zoe was certain she hadn't made any noise. She considered slipping off back into her own room but a curious fascination held her.

She entered Kate's room. Her grandmother was propped up by pillows on her bed, staring blankly off into space, disengaged from the world. Zoe noted the large antique chest at the foot of the bed, its surface piled with afghans and colorful quilts. They reminded her of those she had in her own room back home. She'd never asked where they'd come from. Was it possible her grandmother had sent them and she'd never been told?

Zoe glanced back at the older woman in her old sleigh bed. What was going on behind those light blue eyes? Did her grandmother have a clue her granddaughter was in the room, or was she just out there somewhere—untouchable? Spooked, Zoe hurried to turn out the light as Kate had asked so she could make her escape. As she reached for the lamp by the side of the bed, a weathered hand appeared, gently intercepting her own. Startled, Zoe stared down into the eyes of her grandmother.

"Do I know you?" Kate asked hesitantly.

"Um," Zoe stammered, biting her lip. She turned and eyed the door, imagining herself racing through it. But her hand was pulled closer until she was once again facing the stranger in the bed.

"Sometimes I can't always—" Her grandmother broke off, her face a map of confusion.

Zoe stared at her. What was she supposed to say now? Where was her father? He should be here dealing with this. Yet as Zoe continued to look into the aged, searching face she felt herself drawn to the frustration and the ache she saw there.

Kate moved her fingers side to side across her lips as if mulling over some riddle. And then a light flickered.

"Zoe, is it?" Kate ventured softly.

Zoe's lips parted in surprise. "Yes," she responded tentatively.

"Good," Kate said with the pleasure of a schoolchild accustomed to always getting the answers wrong who, at long last, had gotten one right.

Zoe held her breath. It appeared to her that having worked out some piece of a puzzle, the frail lady was now withdrawing into herself. She watched in stunned silence as the gleam of recognition in her grandmother's face faded away right before her eyes. Kate silently turned over onto her side and closed her eyes.

Zoe felt like crying. Was that all she was going to get? From her own grandmother? As she returned to her own room, emotions swirled inside her like undertows, threatening to suck her down and drown her. She didn't want to care. Not about this old woman or her father or even her mother, who was off on a *real* vacation.

A familiar pain took hold as Zoe stood silently in the dark. She'd never been able to give voice to it. Not in a way that any adult could understand. She walked over to her backpack, which sat in the corner of the room beside a metal heating grate. Digging into the pack, she scrounged around until she found what she was looking for. She pulled out a pair of small silver scissors; calmly she rolled up her left sleeve and stared down at several crude, thin, red flesh carvings that encircled her arm like scratched-in bracelets.

A pale moonlight poured softly into the room as Zoe carefully lined one of the sharp metal points alongside the freshest marking on her arm and began methodically to notch her emotions on the canvas of her skin.

14

How are those numbers looking?" Teddy quipped on his cell to Judith as he drove into town the next morning. "I better get some bump from this trip because I'm here a day and a half and it's gruesome." He slowed to keep from hitting a family of quail making their way across the road and saw them disappear into the brush.

"Keep it together, kiddo. This is a home run. How's that mother of yours doing anyway?"

Teddy pursed his lips. "She's . . . it's pretty weird. What can I say?"

"What about the daughter?" Judith queried, sounding pre-occupied.

Teddy shook his head. "I'm on my way to find her something to do for the next few days. Believe me, it's all about self-preservation." He groaned, turning at the rotary and heading for town. "I wanted to connect with her. Doesn't appear that's going to happen."

"Hey," his campaign manager responded with the enthusiasm of one who hadn't heard a word. "At least you're getting some quality time with her, huh?"

Teddy flinched as a scooter shot by him. "Yeah. Thanks. Anyway, get the staff to e-mail me the background files for the debate. I'll look them over."

"Getting in any *multitasking* while you're on the island?" Judith teased. "I mean, there must be candidates. There are always candidates."

"No, I'm not *multitasking* anyone, but I definitely should be," Teddy insisted. "Don't worry, if I do get a chance, you'll never hear about it."

"I'd just remind you of two little words," his campaign manager said coldly. *"Bill Clinton."*

"Like that would ever stop me," he quipped. "Listen, I'm giving Joanna one week tops, then I'm phoning that we're out of here. What's she going to do, right?"

"Don't forget," Judith insisted. "Get me a good photo of you and your mother. We're going to run it like hell."

"You're a damn mercenary, you know that?" Teddy said with a shake of his head. "Okay, go. Spin. Bye."

As he entered town, Teddy gazed at the berths filled with magnificent yachts and fishing vessels. His stomach started to churn when he passed Old North Wharf with its nestle of shingled cottages. And then, he was there. He hadn't planned to park near Steamboat Wharf, it had just happened. As he got out, Teddy's hands were sweating. Slowly, he crossed the last few yards to the edge of the pier.

Teddy stared down at the choppy water lapping the pillars. Here, on a fog-filled August night, his father had died. Richard Mathison, escaping yet another bitter fight with Kate, had gone for a drive. She was always riding him about something, insisting that his job as a bank executive wasn't paying the bills. How he was draining the life out of her, how she had to paint. Teddy remembered their arguing that awful night—the desperation in his father's voice and his mother's steely disdain—then he'd heard the door slam. Having had too much to drink, his father became disoriented in an unusually heavy midnight fog and ran out of road at the end of Steamboat Wharf. When an arriving ferry brimming with summer visitors collided with the car the next day, it was dredged out and his father's body was discovered in the driver's seat.

The water moved. But as he continued to fixate on a spot where the sunlight played across its surface, Teddy could swear an image was forming. Another memory: his father looking over his shoulder as he attempted a still life in the studio.

"You're wasting your time, Teddy," he heard his father say in his deep baritone. "You should be out playing ball like the other kids. Getting into trouble. Art is for girls." Teddy was nine then and painting every day. He remembered feeling he was letting his father down and had made it a point to paint only when his dad was up in Boston during the week.

"The world understands influence and money. You get one, you'll have the other," Richard Mathison liked to say. "That's when you know you've made something of yourself."

Teddy thought of the pride his father would have felt seeing his son on the campaign trail now. A sharp pain coursed through his chest.

He glanced up and saw a ferry teeming with visitors drawing closer to its berth right where he stood. Looking back down, he could no longer find the spot in the water where his father died. The light had moved on. The image washed away.

His mother was responsible for all of this, he knew. But he had to shake himself from this mood or it would swallow him. Turning up Broad Street, he set out to find a distraction for Zoe. And, if he was lucky, maybe even for himself.

15

Striding around the corner onto Federal Street minutes later, Teddy practically fell into the tiny Nantucket Visitor's Center. A rosy-cheeked woman in her seventies looked up from her place behind the counter. "Can I help you?" she asked.

Teddy scanned the multitude of pamphlets and handouts stacked before him. "I'm looking for some kind of summer program for teens. Just for the week," he said.

The woman quickly and efficiently gathered up every brochure she could lay her hands on.

"What's this . . . ?" Teddy asked, staring at the formidable bundle.

"You got the whole works there, fella. Knock yourself out."

Just as he was reaching for them, Teddy's cell rang. The old matron stared grimly. Teddy got the hint and raced out the door to answer the phone. Distracted, he plowed into a woman making her way into the center, knocking her to the ground and sending her belongings scattering across the sidewalk. In the collision of their bodies Teddy's phone flew from his hand, continuing its haranguing ring.

"There a fire somewhere?" the woman asked, without looking up.

"I'm really sorry," Teddy replied, kneeling down to retrieve his phone and help her pick up papers with his free hand, speaking into the cell. "Joanna, what's . . . ?" His face contorted at his sister's inhospitable response. "Whoa. Hold it right . . . I don't care what . . ."

He found he was nearly cheek to cheek with an attractive derriere and quickly deduced it would be criminal to ignore it. As his sister went on and on, chastising him for paying off the caretaker in order to shirk his responsibilities, Teddy's mind was elsewhere.

"Yeah, Jo, you're right," he said in a sudden hurry. "I'll phone you. Gotta go." He flipped the phone shut and called out to the woman. "Here, let me get that . . ."

"I've got it," she insisted, recovering the last of her papers. Getting to her feet, she turned to him, wiping the auburn hair from her eyes. Teddy recognized her.

"Hey," he remarked, surprised. "You were our waitress from yesterday. Liza, right?"

"Right," she said, occupied with pulling her things together.

"You okay?" Teddy studied her with elaborate concern. "Didn't break anything, did you?"

She looked back at him with amusement. "They grow us hardy on the island," she asserted, moving to hang her poster on the door of the visitor's center. "Here, hold this," she said, handing him a large wheel of masking tape. She tore off a hunk, turning back to finish putting up her advertisement.

For a moment Teddy forgot his mission to find an activity for Zoe. He couldn't help but notice Liza's striking, deep blue eyes. Her hair, free of its ponytail, tumbled into ringlets framing her face. She had delicate high cheekbones and, Teddy noted, fair skin that was flawless and makeup free. He figured her to be in her late thirties. As he stood there checking the woman out, he found himself recalling Zoe's rules. Which one was he breaking now?

"You think maybe I could buy you a coffee? Make it up to you for causing you all this trouble." He grinned smoothly, turning up the charm. "I mean, when you think about it, people meet for a reason, right?"

She barely suppressed her laughter.

Teddy's smooth-operator switch fizzled. Was she brushing him off?

"We haven't really met. Liza Swain," she said, extending her hand.

"Teddy Mathison," he offered, checking for a sign of recognition. Perhaps she'd seen him in the paper or on the news? But the woman seemed to have no idea who he was.

"Wait a minute," Liza said, her face lighting up.

Here it is, Teddy told himself, reassured. Now we're getting somewhere.

"Are you any relation to Kate Mathison, the artist?"

Teddy bit his lip. "Uh, yeah," he confirmed without enthusiasm. "She's my mother."

"Wow. You're so lucky. She's amazing," Liza said, duly impressed. "When I was growing up on the island people treated her like royalty. They used to call your mom 'the Queen of Nantucket.'"

Teddy didn't respond.

"Guess that would make you the prince, huh?" she suggested impishly.

"Actually, I'm running for the Senate. From California," Teddy interjected, hoping to change the subject.

"Oh," Liza said, as if he'd just told her he was a trash collector. Or worse.

"Well," she went on, "since you're related to a great artist I'm going to let you off with a warning for plowing into me." She grinned. "Slow down. We hand out tickets on the island for people in a hurry."

Teddy gave her his best hangdog look.

"Let me guess," she said, shaking her head. "You're used to women saying yes when you ask them out after knocking them over?"

"Well, yeah." He smiled boyishly.

"Maybe that works for you in L.A."

Why wasn't he getting through to this woman?

Liza noted the brochures he'd picked up at the visitor's center. "Looking for something for your daughter to do?" She handed him one of her own flyers. "Photography. I provide the cameras and film. I show kids the island, a little bit about technique, and they shoot what they want."

"Really," Teddy said approvingly. "So you're not just, um, well . . ."

She gazed back, amused. "A waitress?" she deadpanned. "No, we islanders can do a lot of things. We're real multitaskers."

Teddy looked up, surprised, and burst into laughter.

"Something funny?"

"No, it's just . . . ," he stammered. "Never mind." He scanned the brochure, shaking his head. "I don't know, this doesn't sound like Zoe."

Liza looked as if she'd heard this kind of skepticism before. "They aren't so good with words sometimes, kids. But with pictures . . ." Liza paused, her eyes coming alive with passion. "They find a way to tell their story. So give it some thought. We start the new session this Wednesday at nine. We still have a few open slots. Even if it's only for a few days." She waved and started off down the street.

"Hey, how about that coffee?" Teddy tried once again.

"Come up with a better line next time and we'll see," she called back as she turned the corner at India Street and disappeared.

His cell jumped again and, frustrated, he grabbed for it. "Joanna, I really can't—"

"Teddy?" It was Frank's worried voice that came through instead. "You better get yourself back here right away . . ."

"Is Zoe giving you a hard time?" Teddy snapped. "Frank, I swear she's—"

"Not Zoe," the older man interrupted, sounding out of breath. "It's your mother . . ."

16

Bounding up the steps into the house, Teddy called out but got no response. Suddenly, a commotion coming from the back of the house caught his attention and he bolted for the art studio, halting just inside its doorway.

His mother was standing before her unfinished canvas in a dressing gown, her sleeves drawn up, her arms bare. Her left arm was marked with three distinct paint samples squeezed from their tubes, rendering her skin a palette. In her right hand she held a brush dripping cobalt blue. Annie stood a few feet from her, a towel in her arm, looking on anxiously as Frank quietly entreated Kate to hand him the brush and sit down.

"Teddy-boy," Frank acknowledged, trying his best to keep things calm. "Maybe you can give us a hand here, eh?"

"She's been out of sorts all morning," Annie whispered in Teddy's direction. "I haven't seen her like this before. She just doesn't want to listen, poor thing."

Teddy slowly approached his mother. She stared back suspiciously as if he were a stranger intent on stealing from her.

"Mix the colors carefully," she mumbled to no one in particular. "No one ever seems to get it right," she snapped, dabbing more of the oil paint onto a bare patch of skin.

"Come now, Kate," Frank urged gently. "Let's put those things down and have ourselves a bit of a rest."

The older woman smiled mischievously. "The dawn is red, turned on its head, away, away the morning . . . ," she sang softly.

Teddy recognized the lullaby she used to sing to him as a boy. He stood transfixed. She was so alive, even unhinged like this. Watching her mixing paint in this bizarre manner was mesmerizing, if maddening.

"You'll want your tea, Mrs. Mathison," Annie offered, taking a step closer, readying the towel to clean Kate off.

But Kate didn't appear to hear her. Instead, she turned to face her unfinished canvas on the easel and raised her brush to apply the paint she had prepared.

"No," Frank called out. "Now don't go touching your painting, Kate. Tell her, Teddy. She's going to go and ruin what she's already done there. If she were in her right mind, she'd never forgive herself."

"Let her paint," Teddy said.

"Teddy . . . ," Frank cautioned, almost begging.

"Annie," Teddy asked, his eyes remaining on Kate. "Is there any chance this Alzheimer's could reverse itself and allow my mother to recover the skills she once had?"

"Well, no. I don't think so . . . ," the woman responded hesitantly. "The doctors say you can maybe slow the progress with drugs, which she's been taking," the hefty woman offered, wiping perspiration from her face. "But they tell me there's no going back."

"Right," Teddy replied with a shrug. "You hear that, Frank? She'll never finish the thing. There's no market for a half-completed painting. So I say, let her have at it. Go on, Kate," Teddy drew closer, challenging her. "Paint your brains out."

"Teddy," Frank objected. "What in God's name are you doing?"

Teddy ignored Frank's concern. "Who are you right now, Mom?" he whispered in her ear. "Do we have the real Kate, the self-absorbed destroyer of lives, or the sweet, befuddled imposter?"

"Teddy . . . ," the Irishman cautioned, but to no avail.

"Let's take a look at what you have here," Teddy said, moving alongside Kate and appraising the colors on her arm. "Hmm. Naphthol Scarlet, by the looks of it—the 'modern-day vermilion,' isn't that what you used to call it? Excellent choice, Kate," he pronounced, guiding her toward the canvas. "Go ahead—knock yourself out."

"Your mother was always good to you," Frank objected. "She's not here for your amusement."

"Tell that to Richard Mathison." Teddy shook his head, growing more agitated. "No matter how hard he worked for his family, he never could seem to measure up in the eyes of the great artist. He was never good enough, was he, Kate?"

"You've got that all wrong, I'm telling you, Teddy," Frank countered, making a move to reason with him.

Ignoring the older man, Teddy watched the smile growing on his mother's face and, for a brief moment, the anger faded and he was a boy again, thrilled, despite himself, at seeing her approach her canvas, brush in hand. But the hurt inside him would not be stilled.

"Lay it on, Kate," he coaxed. "Paint whatever you want. What difference does it make?"

"Leave her alone," came a loud voice from the corner.

Teddy turned to find Zoe advancing on him in a rage, her eyes focused with determination.

"Zoe," Teddy warned, his face reddening. "Stay out of it. You have no idea what this is about."

"I know that she's an old woman and she's sick. But as sick as she is, you're worse, Dad. You pick on people who can't defend themselves. Is that the way you were in court? Is that your plan for the election, to bully your way into office?"

"Zoe . . . ," Teddy objected.

But his daughter was relentless. "You don't know how to treat anyone. Whatever she did, she's a person. You don't get that, do you?" Zoe's eyes challenged him with defiance. "No wonder you don't know how to be a father," she declared. "You're totally clueless as a son."

Teddy stood there staring into his daughter's eyes. He glanced over at Frank, whose expression told him to let it go. Annie stood, shaking and confused, without the slightest idea what she was in the middle of. Kate continued to mix colors on her arms, glancing up distractedly.

Zoe looked down at her father's hands, which were clenched in frustration. "What, are you going to hit me?" she said.

"Of course not," Teddy replied, stunned at her words. He unclenched his hands.

A loud shriek silenced the room. Everyone turned toward Kate, who stood staring at her arms in dismay. "How in the hell did I get covered in all of this?" she called out, pivoting from her canvas to face her son. "Answer me, someone?"

"Mrs. Mathison, why don't we . . . ?" Annie took the brush and tried leading her over to a chair but Kate would have none of it.

"Who put this damn paint on my arms?" she railed stubbornly.

"Ah, the imperious queen returns," Teddy quipped. He pointed to her unfinished canvas. "You did it to yourself, Mother," he explained calmly. "You were just going to paint your masterpiece, Kate. Go ahead. Have at it."

Kate looked at him and then at the unfinished painting on the easel, her forehead wrinkled with outrage. "I was not going to paint," she stammered. "Why would you say such a thing? Frank, why would he say that? I can't . . . trust my hands. I would never . . ." She turned, breathing hard, staring at Annie, Zoe, Frank, and Teddy distrustfully. "Here, what are you all doing? Who's responsible for this?"

"Katie, take it easy," Frank soothed.

"Don't tell me to take it easy, Frank Lafferty," she snapped.

"*You* are responsible," Teddy reported. "You. It's always been you."

"What are you babbling about, Teddy?" she demanded, growing frustrated.

"You can't just bully people around anymore, Mom," Teddy announced.

"It's the Alzheimer's talking," the Irishman insisted. "Don't pay it any mind."

"Bullshit," Teddy blurted. "This is exactly how I remember her. Ordering people. This is the way she spoke to my father. Remember, Kate? This is how you treated Richard Mathison." He was winding up, face reddening, the anger that had always been there welling up.

Kate turned to face her son and blinked at the sound of the name. "Richard was my husband." She squinted through the clouds in her brain. "What do you know about it?"

"I know that you bullied him whenever he was home," Teddy fired off. "Which wasn't that often, thanks to you. Why wasn't he ever around for long, Mom? Ever ask yourself that? Ever figure it out?"

Kate erupted in defiance. "Words. Words. Words. Enough out of you, Richard," she scolded, marching on him.

"Richard?! What the hell . . . ?" Teddy shook his head in confusion.

"Kate . . . ," Frank cautioned. "This is Teddy. Your son."

"My son?" The older woman looked at him, puzzled, reaching out for a nearby chair to steady herself. "My son doesn't visit me," she insisted, piecing it out in her mind. "He's like you, Richard," she said, turning to Teddy. "He stays away."

Teddy slammed his hand against the back of the wooden chair, anger and hurt bubbling up from deep within him. "How, Mother, can you expect someone to stay in the picture when there's no room left for anyone *but* the artist?"

Like a stubborn child, Kate put her hands to her ears.

In frustration, Teddy went to her, pulling her hands away. He would force her to listen.

"Teddy!" Frank cried out, moving to pull him off.

"Daddy, no!" Zoe screamed.

But Teddy pressed on. "You were the one. You're why he got lost out there that night. You made his life miserable. Admit it, Kate!"

Annie held her breath. "My God."

"You were the one who drove him to it," Teddy howled as the others stood frozen in the wake of his ferocity. "The man had nowhere else to turn but the bottle. There was no *give* in you. You were always tearing him down when you should have been building him up. And now, now, Kate, with your impeccable sense of timing, you go and get Alzheimer's so you don't have to face any of it. But I know the truth. *You* killed him."

Teddy stood over her, beet red, his breathing labored.

Kate gave a little gasp. "Paint me a picture, Teddy?" She blinked, giving him a sad little smile. "Paint me a picture of what you see . . ."

"No, Mom. No, I won't paint for you," he spat, backing her up as Frank moved to come between them.

"Dad. Stop it!" Zoe called out, grabbing hold of him from behind. As she did, Teddy stumbled awkwardly sideways. Catching his breath, Frank helped Kate into a chair. Annie threw herself into the task of cleaning the paint off the old woman's arms.

Recovering, Teddy was relentless. "I gave up painting long ago, and you know the hell why. It was you, Kate." His finger jabbed the air. "You. Do you hear me?! *I didn't want to be anything like you.*"

Slowly, from her chair, Kate lifted her head, looking at her son with a sudden clarity that seared him.

"But Teddy," she said with the softness of a mother he'd never known. "You can never give up on what you love."

17

Their bags were packed and out on the front steps. He had phoned Judith the night before to let her know they were coming back sooner than expected. "Good," she had replied firmly. "Hoyt and Emerson are having a heyday with you out of state. I know I pushed for the family photo op, but nothing beats pressing the flesh and being available for the cameras. I'll call a press conference so we can get some airplay. I hope you have that damn photograph of you and your mother. That's gold, Teddy. Gold."

Now, standing on the front porch with the luggage, he eyed several boards that needed replacing. He flipped open his phone and called his sister and, over her vehement protests, stated the imperative of his return to California. "You don't like it, Jo, well, you run for office and let me know how much time you have to sit with dear old mom." He hung up. He considered his obligation fulfilled.

Teddy went back inside to find Annie and say good-bye. Because of the incident in the studio the day before, she was cool to him. That didn't stop Teddy from pressing a hundred-dollar bill into her hand. Looking around the house for his daughter, he discovered Zoe in the last place he expected—the art studio. She was sitting off to the side, her eyes fixed on her dozing grandmother.

"Fifteen minutes," Teddy announced.

Zoe didn't bother to look up. To Teddy's surprise, she hadn't reacted well when he'd stuck his head in her room that morning to let her know they were leaving. He'd thought she'd be relieved to get out of there. But since she wasn't speaking to him anyway, Teddy figured she could do that just as well back in L.A. Glancing over at Kate, he suddenly remembered the photo he needed. Pulling his cell phone out, he flipped it open and clicked the camera button, smiling boyishly at Zoe.

"What do you want?" Zoe eyed him suspiciously.

"A photo with my mother. Would you do the honors?" he asked, holding out the cell.

"Aren't you at least going to wake her up?" she asked icily.

"Why? There's no reason to disturb her. I'll just put my arms around her and rest her head against my shoulder. That will look sweet, don't you think?"

"I don't believe you," Zoe spat and bolted from the room.

Kneeling beside his sleeping mother, Teddy could hear her raspy, labored breathing. He felt a slight twinge of guilt at what he was about to do but then reminded himself that Kate would be ruthless if she needed something to further *her* career.

"Here's to all the good times, huh, Mom?" he whispered without emotion. And, with one arm extended, holding the cell camera in front of them, he leaned next to her and snapped several shots. Getting up, he checked to be sure he had at least one nice picture. Satisfied that he had something his staff could download, he pressed Save, snapped off the camera function, and, glancing down one last time, quickly turned and left his mother behind.

Frank waited for him on the front porch. There was something odd about the man. His eyes looked almost fearful and he appeared pale and spent, as if he'd been up all night.

"If you plan on lecturing me, Frank, you can save it," Teddy said, trying to sound upbeat as he lugged the bags over to the convertible to load up.

After tucking the bags in the trunk, Teddy headed back in to get Zoe, but Frank blocked the way, saying nothing.

"Look, I'm sorry for the way things worked out, but I do appreciate all you've done for my family," Teddy said gently. "Now I've got to get Zoe or we'll miss our flight."

As Teddy tried to slip past him Frank's arm held him back.

"There's something you don't . . . I mean maybe you should—" Frank broke off, his voice trembling.

Teddy put his hand on the older man's shoulder and turned to face him. He saw the curious way Frank's gaze seemed to tighten as his lips pursed to say words that never came. As he watched, the energy seemed to drain out of the Irishman. Instead, he simply shook his head.

"Good-bye, Teddy," Frank said, slowly and sadly. He stared deeply into Teddy's eyes, then turned and walked to his car and pulled away.

Teddy stood there looking after him for a moment. It occurred to him that this might be the last time he would ever see the older man. Maybe that's what Frank had been trying to express. It might have been the reason he came over. Still, the explanation didn't quite fit. It was bizarre. Teddy shook his head and turned back to the house to get his daughter.

He was just inside the door when he stopped cold. His heart nearly skipped a beat as he pivoted back outside and peered down the road after the older man's car. That look in Frank's eyes. He knew that look. It was more than the sadness of a *good-bye*. There had been fear there, he realized, and, more important, the need to unburden himself. He stood in the doorway, staring in the direction Frank's car had gone. The lawyer in Teddy told him that whatever Frank was holding on to was important. So important that the old man had somehow been unable to tell him even though he wanted to. Whatever it was or however it might impact him, Teddy knew he couldn't leave without finding out. Without a word to Annie or Zoe, he got into his car and tore out of the driveway.

Speeding along Polpis Road, Teddy spied the old station wagon and flashed his lights to get Frank's attention. The older man didn't respond and, in frustration, Teddy hit the gas to catch up with him. Drawing alongside, he signaled for Frank to pull over. To his surprise, the old man pulled away. Teddy's suspicions were verified. A chill went through him as he maneuvered his Infiniti behind Frank's car. He honked the horn for Frank to pull over. Still the Irishman refused. Frustrated, adrenaline pumping, Teddy swerved his car into the left lane of the two-lane road and drew alongside the station wagon again.

"Pull over, Frank," he shouted. "I need to talk to you!"

But Frank just increased his speed. The two tore down the rustic road past Sesachacha Pond like teen drag racers on a dare, each waiting for the other to back down. Suddenly, an island transit bus came barreling around a bend straight for him, and Teddy was forced to hit the brakes and fall back behind the Irishman's station wagon. Then, slipping into high gear, he pulled to Frank's right, inadvertently forcing the old man into the oncoming traffic lane. Panic gripped the Irishman as he swerved around the bend and saw a sanitation truck bearing down on him, its horn blaring.

Teddy stopped breathing as the vehicle bore down on Frank's car. At the last moment the older man managed to turn sharply back into the lane in front of Teddy. Both cars kicked up gravel as the wheels treaded the bumpy surface of the road shoulder before spilling onto a dirt lot.

Rushing out of the convertible, Teddy scrambled toward the station wagon. "Are you out of your mind? What the hell's wrong with you?!" he screamed in shock.

Frank had a hand over his heart, staring wildly up at Teddy. "What's wrong with *me*?! You nearly got me killed," the old man roared back.

"I was desperate to get you to stop, because you wanted to tell me something. And then you didn't. I have a feeling it's something I need to know."

The older man fidgeted in his seat. "Jesus, why didn't you just leave, go back to where you came from. You're hot to go, right?" He rubbed his right eye with the palm of his hand as he spoke, his voice sad. "So go, get out of here!"

And then Teddy noticed the way the old man kept glancing to his right as if searching for something. That's when Teddy saw an envelope on the floor of the car. He and Frank went after it at the same time. The two wrestled a moment before Teddy managed to pry it from the old man's hands and draw away. The Irishman pulled himself from the car just as Teddy was turning the envelope over in his hands. The intended recipient's name was written in a messy scrawl that he recognized from his childhood; it read, *To Kate.*

The older man leaned against the car, as though exhausted, as Teddy pulled out a piece of yellowed paper. The writing was his father's, he was certain of it.

Frank gazed at his own hands and spoke sadly. "A long time ago she made me promise to destroy it. Your mother couldn't. She said they were Richard's last words and she couldn't bring herself to burn the note. But I held on to it all these years. I wasn't sure why. I shouldn't have come by this morning . . . shouldn't have brought the letter. That's why I tried to get away from you. I knew if you stopped me, I'd give it to you."

Teddy had never heard anyone sound so heartbroken. He patted Frank on the shoulder gently and began to read.

> *Kate,*
>
> *There is no good way to apologize for what I've put you through so I won't try: the women, the money I lost, the drinking. The kids were lucky you were there for them through all my mistakes. I wanted to be something, Katie. I just never found what it was. You tried to help me, but*

*that just made me leave you every chance I had, which, in
turn, made you angry, of course. I made your life miserable.
I know that. And now I'm going to make it simpler and,
I suppose, more complicated at the same time.*

Good-bye, my darling.

Richard

Teddy felt as if a knife had pierced his heart. He gasped for
breath and his mind reeled as the paper dropped from his hands.

"Your mother never wanted you to see this," Frank con-
fessed, shaking his head. "Up in Connecticut, where she is from,
people of her generation keep things like this quiet. The shame
of it, you know, and she knew how much you looked up to your
father. She didn't want to take that away from you," he said
sadly. "It was at her own expense, I warned her, but she swore me
to secrecy, the dear, stubborn woman."

Teddy stared at Frank, trying to fully comprehend what the
note and the older man's words meant. Numb, he walked slowly
to his car. The sound he heard in his head was that of a belief sys-
tem imploding. His father hadn't died in an accident. Richard
Mathison had taken his own life.

Teddy placed the key in the ignition. Frank was yelling
something at him, but the words didn't register. He pulled out
onto the road. For reasons he didn't understand, he was drawn
back to Sconset. He drove by the open heathlands, their tall
grasses swaying in the summer breeze. He whizzed past the
moors off to the right with their array of vegetation and expan-
sive views. He saw none of it. Off to his left, across a newly built

golf course, the Sankaty Head Lighthouse, ever on duty, flashed its beacon of warning as if meant for him alone.

Turning into the driveway, Teddy was accosted by Zoe, who stood on the steps screaming—something about why had he left her and was he out of his mind or what?—but he couldn't deal with her anger just now. Staring up at the house, he wanted to run in and demand that his mother explain why she had kept the news of his father's suicide from him. But instead he was astounded at how different the house suddenly seemed, as if he had never known it at all. Stumbling backward, Teddy turned and jogged alongside the lighthouse, over the bluff, and straight down the trail to the place he always went when he was in trouble: the ocean.

Running out onto the beach, he felt as if every molecule in his body would burst. Teddy stared out to sea, his breathing ragged, his heart on fire. All a lie, he kept repeating to himself. He had built his entire life on a lie. His father was not the man he had fiercely protected and admired.

As the waves crashed against the shore, Teddy fought to catch his breath. His knees buckled and, slowly, he crumpled to the sand.

The women, the money I lost, the drinking. Kate hadn't caused his father's death. Richard Mathison had made that choice for himself.

18

*T*alk to me, Teddy pleaded.

The memory emerged from deep inside him.

The sea lapped the sand, its gentle rhythm soothing to a young boy's ears. On the beach, maybe fifty yards away, a man lifted his head. It was his father. The boy ran to him for a hug but, all at once, drew back. There was a strange look in his dad's eyes. A bad smell on his breath that Teddy didn't recognize. An empty bottle lay nearby. "Sorry," his father muttered, eyes big and sad and scary. "So sorry. So, so, so, so sorry," he repeated, slurring his words, tossing his arms helplessly like a wounded bird. Suddenly, he collapsed and began to cry into the sand. The boy felt a heat in his cheeks and an ache in his chest. Something was wrong, something terrible had happened.

Shaking, he sat down next to his father and patted his back while he stared out at the water. Make my father better, he silently begged. Make what hurts go away.

Teddy abruptly lifted his head. He wasn't sure how long he had been lying there in the sand, but he became aware of an urgent voice calling his name. It felt as though he was dreaming, but the voice was growing ever more frantic. He turned and saw a small, dark figure, her arms waving wildly, standing on the bluff above him. It was Zoe and she looked panic-stricken. His heart froze.

Something terrible had happened.

Charging hard up from the beach and sprinting around the front of the house, Teddy was stunned to find his mother being lifted into the bay of an EMT vehicle. Her unconscious body seemed small and unprotected, laid out on the stretcher and partially covered with a blanket.

Zoe was on the curb now, bouncing restlessly on her heels and looking forlorn and anxious. Frank had pulled up and was standing in the road, watching. He took out a red handkerchief and mopped his brow, eyes fixed on Kate, before turning and getting back in his car, ready to follow the ambulance.

"She collapsed in the studio," Annie explained, her voice trembling, as Teddy stopped at her side, his heart racing.

One of the EMTs looked up. "You folks can follow in the car." He pointed to Frank's station wagon.

The red light atop the emergency vehicle flashed in Teddy's eyes. He walked forward and began to climb into the ambulance.

"Wait a minute. What do you think you're doing?" A barrel-chested medical tech had his hand on Teddy's elbow.

"I'm going . . . with her," Teddy replied, finding his voice.

"You a member of the family?"

Teddy looked down at the unconscious body of his mother, the words catching in his throat.

"I'm her son."

19

It was all a whir—the lightning ride to the Nantucket Cottage Hospital, siren blaring; rushing in alongside the stretcher until a nurse barred him from the emergency room; the pacing in the corridor as he gazed into the troubled faces of Frank, Annie, and Zoe. He couldn't be sure but he thought he'd placed a hand on his daughter's shoulder and she had let it stay there for more than a moment. And then the doctor came out to talk to them.

"She's stable," the middle-aged physician, Dr. Jennings, assured them as they stood under the dim lights of the corridor. "Kate experienced what we might call a ministroke and took a hard spill, but there was no concussion. With forms of dementia, like Alzheimer's, we often find that as the mind progressively shuts down, the body follows."

"What are you saying, Doctor? She's going to have more strokes?" Teddy asked.

"Could be. But I doubt it. From my examination, she's weakening. She's in the middle stages. You may find flashes of memory, even complete lucidity at times, but it will vanish again, like a ghost of her former self."

The doctor spoke directly to Teddy. "I've been seeing your mother the last few summers so I've followed this progression," he said. "Her body is simply slowly giving out."

"But she has to have more time . . . I need more time with her." Teddy's words surprised everyone.

From her post against the drab green wall, Zoe drew nearer, studying her father's face.

The doctor shook his head sadly. "Time, I'm afraid, is her enemy."

Without a word, Teddy turned and walked through the emergency doors and out into the open air. Stunned at the discovery of his father's suicide, he was filled with remorse. He'd always blamed his mother. Now he knew his father had cheated on her, hurt her, and lied to his kids. Who was she, this mother of his? He'd spent a lifetime hating her and not really knowing her. How could he ever make up for that? How could he slice through the fog clouding her brain and tell her he was sorry? Was it possible to find her, before it was too late? As he stood there torn between guilt and uncertainty, there was one thing he knew he had to do. Taking out his cell phone, Teddy hit Judith's number.

"Judith," he said. "I'm not leaving just yet."

"I've already put out a press release," she snapped, enraged. "Don't screw around, Teddy. You could lose this nomination. I'm serious. Time is critical."

"Yeah," Teddy muttered, glancing back at the hospital, "I know it is."

20

When Kate returned from the hospital, Teddy was by her side every moment he could be: sitting by her bed, passing hours opposite her in the art studio, lending his arm as he led her for some fresh air and a view of the ocean. He had despised his mother for so long that this compulsion to be near her was overwhelming. Stripped of the certainty about her guilt that had anchored his life, Teddy was adrift in a sea of confusion and unanswered questions.

Willing to believe the worst of his mother, he had drawn a map for his life long ago based on faulty coordinates. The consequences of that mistake were mind-boggling. Having lost one parent as a boy, he had chosen to lose the other as a young man. Career decisions, the choice of a wife who would *not* be like his mother, his entire life's geography, Zoe raised without a grandparent from his family's side—there were so many eventualities, large and small, that his head could not yet fathom—all had been shaped by a judgment he had long ago set in stone and stubbornly refused to reconsider.

He knew he had a brief window of time. Judith made it clear that if he remained off the campaign trail longer than a week he could kiss the nomination good-bye. In addition, his ex wanted Zoe back in eight days for a planned visit to Seattle to see her parents. Having startled his vacationing sister with his plans to stay longer, he was caught off guard by her profound gratitude. It was as if he had rescued Joanna, at least temporarily. Teddy now understood that his mother's hold on reality and life was truly tenuous, that if he was going to come to know her at all, he would have to do it as she was in the process of vanishing.

Teddy began taking mental snapshots.

There was his mother breaking her afternoon-long silence by suddenly shouting, "Red, red, the boat on its side, boat on its side, red, red!" Then she would laugh like a girl before withdrawing into herself. He observed the longing looks she gave her uncompleted painting, her pupils appearing to focus before turning flat and dark like the damaged lens of a camera.

Sitting vigil by her bedside, he was astonished to find her waking from a nap making the sweet gurgling sounds of a newborn. On another occasion she startled him by springing from her chair, pointing to a painting, and joyously labeling it "bluer than blue." He was perplexed and shaken the next day when she began conversing with another artist only she could see.

As he opened himself to the images and sounds of a mother he hadn't allowed himself to know, Teddy struggled and his questions mounted. What was it his father had really been doing all that time off island each summer? Why had he longed for his father's attention when it was his mother and art that he had so admired as a boy? All the fighting between his parents in his youth, could that have actually been the insistence of a proud but brokenhearted woman demanding her husband live up to his obligations and maybe, just maybe, to the promise she saw in him?

Teddy cursed Kate's New England–bred recalcitrance to air the family's dirty laundry, even to her own son. How could she have withheld the truth from him? She was as much to blame for the abyss between them as he was. How different things might have been if Kate had only told him the truth, but she was so incomprehensibly stubborn. Over the next forty-eight hours his mind grappled with it all, shifting from anger to blame, from frustration to sadness. Still, in the middle of the night he lay awake with a nagging question he couldn't answer—why had he chosen to believe the worst of his mother in the first place?

Over the next two days Teddy didn't return the calls he'd found on his cell. He didn't check his e-mail. He fell asleep each night on a sofa in his mother's room. Distracted, he even seemed to forget about Zoe. It was as if Teddy's brain had developed a cloud of its own. He was struggling to piece together some impossible puzzle.

"I'm not sure how I'm supposed to do this," he said on the third day back from the hospital as they sat in the studio. "Make contact. Make things right. You weren't easy, you know?"

Kate was staring at her unfinished painting again.

"I loved my father so much," he murmured. "Did that hurt you?" Teddy stared at the old woman, waiting for an answer.

"Did I love you, too? Is that what you're wondering? Do I love you now?" He inhaled deeply, took a ragged breath, his eyes focusing on his mother's beautiful hands. "I don't know how I feel, except that I wish I had known. I wish you had told me. Can't you . . ." He drew his chair closer and leaned in. "Can't you help me out here, Kate? I want to know you again, Mom." He studied her face, as if he might be able to find some answers there. "There are probably a lot of sons and daughters who could say they don't know their mothers when it comes right down to it. I screwed up, but the thing is, you screwed up, too. Can't you see that?"

Suddenly, Kate turned to him and smiled. "Hello, Teddy," she said, pleasantly surprised. "How are you, son?"

Her voice sounded more fragile than when they'd first arrived, airy and ethereal, like a feather floating on a breeze.

"Mom, I've missed you. I've missed you for so many years. And look, here we are, together. Isn't that something?" He smiled and put his hand on his mother's hand, which was warm, and it surprised him. He could feel her veins through the papery tissue of her skin. Her bones felt delicate and yet there was strength there, too.

Looking in on her father later in the day, Zoe was dumbfounded to find him pouring tea and having a quiet, affectionate conversation with his mother. The next day, she nearly fell over when she found him awkwardly brushing his mother's long white hair. Who *was* this kind imposter? She found her father's sudden, overwhelming attention to her grandmother increasingly irritating. He wasn't acting like the father she knew. Where was all this affection coming from? Why couldn't she have some of it?

That night, as he was helping his mother to bed, the room was hit with a blast of music that made them both gasp. Racing down to the living room, his heart thumping from the sudden shock and the visceral sound of electric bass vibrating throughout the house, Teddy found his daughter locked into her headphones, seemingly oblivious to the fact that the rap she was listening to was simultaneously pouring out of a pair of tiny but deadly travel speakers she'd hooked up.

"Are you out of your mind?" he demanded as he pulled the headphones from her ears and unplugged the speakers.

"Hey, you can't do that to me!" she erupted. "I have rights in this house, too."

"Your grandmother's trying to sleep," Teddy said. "And even if she wasn't, this was loud enough to wake the dead, Zoe."

"What the hell's wrong with you?" she shouted as he turned to leave. "You only care about her now!" she yelled. "You don't give a damn about me."

Teddy pivoted on the stairs, staring back at her. "Don't talk that way," he snapped. "I'm your father and I love you, but your grandmother needs me and that's taking all of my energy right now."

For a moment Zoe looked as if she would cry. Teddy could see the tears brimming in her striking green eyes. Then, calling on a stubbornness he recognized in himself *and* his mother, she lashed out. "This so-called family sucks!" she screamed, flashing a double bird as she ran past him up to her room.

Teddy followed her, but she slammed and locked her door. He stood in the middle of the hallway and let out a long unsettled breath. He had to start over with Zoe. Things weren't good with her, that was for sure.

Later, while getting himself ready for bed, Teddy reached for the informational packet on Alzheimer's that the hospital had given him. Underneath it was a colorful brochure on photography for teens. He had forgotten about this. Picking it up, he recalled the attractive woman he had run into, literally—the one who had turned him down for coffee but admired his mother.

This was what Zoe needed. Other kids her age. Something to occupy her time. He'd call first thing in the morning.

21

Pulling into the dirt parking lot near the Windswept Cranberry Bog off Polpis Road, Teddy glanced over at Zoe brooding in the passenger seat.

"The Nantucket cranberry bogs used to be the biggest in the world," he said, trying to engage her. "It's a great place for photography."

Zoe didn't respond.

"You're going to love it," he said encouragingly.

"You have no idea what I love," she shot back as the car rolled to a stop.

"Hey there," came a welcoming shout from across the lot.

Teddy looked up to find Liza Swain, clipboard in hand, waving enthusiastically. Around her milled a dozen or so teenagers in shorts and T-shirts, chatting one another up as she handed out cameras.

"Come on, Zoe," he entreated his daughter. "Most of these kids are your own age." Getting out, Teddy went around the car and opened the passenger door. "We're going back to L.A. in a week. I've phoned your mom and told her you were going to take this course and she was excited for you." He was getting nowhere with her. "Just try the class, Zoe. It beats sitting around the house. I'll pick you up in five hours when it's over, all right?"

Teddy's eyes flashed from Zoe to the attractive woman looking at them from some thirty feet away, her head cocked, clearly wondering what was keeping them.

"Come on," he hissed. "Don't embarrass me."

"You must be joking, right?" she asked curtly. "*I'm* the embarrassing one? You don't have a clue."

Getting out of the car, Zoe stared disdainfully at the woman waving her forward. "Time out. Isn't that the waitress from town?"

"Yeah. Hey, look at that," Teddy reacted with enthusiasm. "You already know her. Cool."

Zoe glared at the woman. "There is no way I'm following this cheerleader around just 'cause you want to hook up with her," she complained, not caring who heard.

"Damn, Zoe, do you have to talk like that?" Teddy was growing red in the face. "Look, I'm doing this for you . . . you're going to enjoy this," he declared before realizing they had company.

Liza was standing next to the car.

"Hey, you guys. Got your call. You're a few days behind, but you'll catch up, no problem," she enthused. "Zoe, right?"

"Yeah," Zoe mumbled, looking away.

"We met at the Even Keel restaurant. I'm Liza," she said, extending her hand. Zoe shook it weakly.

Liza glanced over at Teddy, who decided to put the best face on things. "She's a little shy around new people," he ventured, giving Liza a conspiratorial wink.

"No, I'm not," Zoe countered, adding under her breath, "How would you know, anyway?"

Changing the subject, Liza turned to Teddy. "How's your mother doing?" she asked. "You mentioned on the phone that her condition is worse."

"It's touch and go. We're just taking it day to day, but thanks for asking." Teddy nodded. With everything on his mind, he still couldn't help noticing that the woman had *great legs*. And that thing with her hair, the cascade of auburn curls. Looking at her made him feel sane again. She was so alive, so healthy and easygoing.

"Hey," he offered, falling back on his habit of charming good-looking women, "in case no one's told you, you look amazing in those shorts. The whole outdoor thing"—he nodded approvingly, flashing an appreciative wink—"it's working for you."

Zoe rolled her eyes and looked away.

"What the hell are you doing?" Liza frowned, slightly incredulous.

The no-nonsense tone snapped Zoe to attention and she gawked at the woman.

"What?" Teddy responded, genuinely not following.

"You know, you have interesting timing, Teddy," she said with a disapproving smile. "I don't think you get it. Those kids over there are waiting." She nodded. "Making some kind of move on me right now, however pathetic, is just totally inappropriate. You get that?"

Zoe's eyes grew wide. She was riveted. No one—except herself, of course—had ever talked to her dad this way. She was used to seeing women fall at his feet. Who was this woman anyhow?

"Whoa, hold on . . . ," Teddy stammered, his face turning crimson. "I was not making a move. When I make a move, believe me, you'll know it. What, we can't give out compliments anymore?" he objected, flashing an embarrassed glance at his daughter, then back to Liza.

Liza gave a knowing smile. "Right, that's what you were doing." She laughed. "Look, just own it." She grinned, shaking her head good-naturedly at Zoe, woman to woman.

The teen smiled back at her, seriously impressed.

Teddy was flabbergasted. With all that was going on he didn't need some PC feminist lecturing him. Who was this waitress-slash-photographer with a mouth? He observed Liza's amused expression; she looked as if she was enjoying his discomfort. Teddy could feel the muscles in his face tightening.

Liza turned to Zoe. "Look, we do a lot of cool things and I'd love for you to be part of the class. Join us or don't, it's your choice, okay?" She smiled warmly. "I've got to get back." With a quick wave at both of them, she hurriedly returned to a group that had grown rowdy in her absence.

Teddy stared after her for a moment, speechless. Insulted, he said, "Come on, Zoe, let's get out of here." He whipped around and headed for the car. Looking over his shoulder for his daughter, he was surprised to find Zoe still standing where he'd left her.

"What are you waiting for?" he said impatiently. "Let's go."

But Zoe stared off in Liza's direction. Her new personal hero was addressing the other teens while focusing the lens of a camera and pointing at the wild shrubbery of the moors behind her. She couldn't help noticing a tall guy, maybe eighteen, who appeared to be helping Liza with the demonstration.

Perplexed, Teddy backtracked to her. "A minute ago I couldn't get you out of the car. Come on, you're right, what does this woman know? She's just someone with an attitude and a camera. Let's go," he urged, exasperated.

His daughter shook her head. "I think I'll stay," she said with a hint of surprise, as if she couldn't quite believe her own decision. "By the way," she added, turning back to him, "like I said before, you don't know much about women."

Taken aback, Teddy watched Zoe make her way over to a dozen or so total strangers. The woman who had just reamed him pretty thoroughly greeted her new student enthusiastically and introduced her all around.

Teddy stared, then slowly returned to his car, his face still flush from the encounter. His daughter's words stung him. He thought of his inability to understand his ex-wife, his mother. He reflected on his struggle to connect to Zoe. And now, there was this maddening woman with great legs and an obvious tendency to lecture. What was her problem? Teddy had to admit he didn't have a clue.

He felt a shiver, as if someone had just told him some unsettling news. Getting behind the wheel of the car, he stared out at Polpis Road, where three young women were racing by on scooters, laughing and beeping their horns.

Could it be, Teddy asked himself incredulously, that he really *didn't* know much about women?

22

Arriving back at the house, Teddy went directly to the downstairs bathroom, found a bottle of Tylenol, and popped several into his mouth.

"I'm sorry you're not feeling well," Annie said in the open doorway.

Teddy jumped. "No, no, I'm fine," he insisted, sounding anything but.

"Good," came the cheery reply. "Then come with me. I need to show you something."

Reluctantly, Teddy followed her up the stairs and down the photograph-lined hallway to his mother's room.

"Occasionally I'll have errands and will need to go out. Later today, for example, I have a doctor's appointment. The point is, you need to know what to do if she has an accident," Annie said, lifting the bedpan from a side table.

"Whoa," Teddy objected, holding his hands up and taking a step back. "That's not something I can do."

Annie gazed back, a quizzical look on her face. "She's sometimes incontinent. At some point she'll need to wear something all the time . . ."

"Diapers?!" Teddy asked with alarm.

"There are special ones for adults," Annie responded calmly. "For now, she can make it to the toilet on her own most of the time. You just need to make sure this is by her bed. I always place it here before I go, but she moves things around and forgets where she's put them."

Teddy stared at her, dumbstruck.

"Look, Annie," he finally said uncomfortably, pressing his hand to his temples. "I have a whole other life that I need to get back to soon and I really don't think I'm going to be of much use in that way. I can't help with things like that. I'm just not cut out for it. I'll pay you double if you'll just see to everything until Joanna gets back. Fair enough?" he all but pleaded. "Can we say we understand each other?"

Annie looked at him coldly. "Mr. Mathison . . ."

"It's Teddy," he insisted, massaging his temple. "People who know me call me Teddy."

The caretaker pursed her lips, taking her measure of him. "I won't deny that I could use the money. But your mother needs her family right now. She won't be around a lot longer and then you won't have to be bothered ever again." She paused, holding his gaze. "You'd be surprised what a little love and dignity will do for someone, especially in your mother's condition," she said pointedly.

"As for you"—she shook her head, a look of pity in her eyes—"my grandmother always said you get to know someone by their actions. Do *we* understand each other, Mr. Mathison?"

Teddy nodded. Suddenly, wherever he went it was like facing an inquisition. "Yes," he mumbled as she walked away.

Heading downstairs, Teddy entered the art studio. He found his mother sitting in her favorite chair. Her eyes were fixed yet again on her uncompleted painting. Suddenly, he felt the whole situation was ludicrous. Here he was running for the United States Senate and he was talking about bedpans and diapers, for Christ's sake!

"It's the light that makes them dance," Kate called out to him in the gentle cadence of a nursery rhyme.

Teddy flinched at the sound of the frail voice. He couldn't get used to not hearing Kate's vibrant, confident tones—the voice of his childhood.

"Red, red . . .," she called out, her eyes locked on the half-completed canvas. "The boat, the boat, the boat on its side . . ."

Was this how Alzheimer's screwed with someone? She was like a mental patient. Teddy had always thought it was simply a matter of losing one's memory. But Kate seemed like a person you might find in a psychiatric ward.

Spellbound, Teddy watched as she lifted her right hand and began stroking the air in front of her as if painting. A pang of sorrow caused Teddy to clench his fists and hold on. Seeing her reduced to this extent was getting to him, and he was forced to turn away. He gazed out the window at the ocean below.

He thought of Liza's humiliating words, his angry daughter's rejection, the sudden revelation about his father, and the sadness of losing a mother he might never truly know.

"Bluer than blue," she whispered. "Make it bluer than blue." She laughed softly. "Bluer than . . ."

Teddy was suddenly besieged by nagging questions. What the hell were all these pronouncements he'd heard the past few days? *It's the light that makes them dance. Red, red, the boat on its side.* Were these fragments of some lost painting? Lullabies his mother remembered from her childhood? And what, Teddy pondered, could possibly exist that was *bluer than blue*?

He looked over at Kate and took a step back. His mother was sitting in her chair absentmindedly running her hands over her breasts. What the hell?

"Annie, are you still here?!"

The chubby caretaker came running into the room, alarmed. She found a flustered Teddy pointing toward his mother.

"Oh, my," she said, taking a deep breath and calming down. "It's the Alzheimer's, poor dear. Makes people do all sorts of odd things." She gently removed Kate's hands and held them in her own to calm her.

Teddy looked away. No one had prepared him for *this*. "What does losing your memory have to do with it?" he stammered in astonishment.

"Boundaries," Annie said, matter-of-factly. "The disease short-circuits them. A censor gets turned off in the head so a person doesn't distinguish between what's private and public."

"What are you doing?" Kate protested, forcing her hands back to her breasts. "Here now, they're mine."

Teddy didn't know whether to laugh or cry. Even lost in her disease, here was his mother, stubborn as always, not to be denied.

"Richard never touches these," Kate announced to no one. Then, discovering Teddy, she grew angry. "Why don't you ever touch these, Richard?" she stammered, confronting him. "They're as good as the ones on the other women you cheat with," she declared.

The declaration embarrassed and saddened Teddy. As Annie calmed his mother and led her upstairs for a bath, he couldn't shake the sobering realization that she was locked off in a world he couldn't comprehend. Since her collapse, her lucid moments were fewer and farther between. But Teddy's questions about his past were like a fishing line hooked under his ribs, pulling him forward. What else didn't he know about his father? Who was his mother really? What had gone on in his parents' marriage?

Teddy knew there was only one person to whom he could turn for answers.

23

Jibbing downwind, Frank maneuvered the stern of his twelve-and-a-half-foot sloop through the eye of the wind. As the boom cut across the boat, Teddy had to duck quickly to avoid being knocked into the water.

"Your instincts are a bit rusty." The older man laughed. "You practically summered on my boat when you were old enough to tie a bowline. Now look at you," he teased, eyes twinkling. "Nothing more than a landlubber."

"Sorry." Teddy grinned. "I forgot what a maniac you are when you get your hand on a rudder."

As they came about, both men were hit with sea spray. The Irishman ran a sleeve across his face. "I'm glad you stayed around," he said, guiding the sailboat westward by Wauwinet.

Teddy nodded, staring out across the expanse of ocean toward Cape Cod.

"Talk about maniacs," Frank joked. "You used to bike over to my place and beg me to take you out in the boat." He smiled.

"One time I'd just returned from visiting my family in Eeyries back in West Cork. I was exhausted, dead to the world. You might as well have moved me straight to the cemetery. But you, all of ten, come bursting through my front door, yammering about some bottleneck whale that'd been spotted off of Coatue and how we had to sail there immediately." He shook his head at the memory. "I felt like walloping you from here to the mainland."

Teddy smiled, wiping the spray out of his eyes. "You took me."

Frank nodded. "Well, you bellyached like a banshee, promising to catch me a couple of bluefish and clean my tackle for a week. You were so pitiful, I gave in, God love me."

"You're a good man, Frank," Teddy acknowledged. "You've been a true friend."

The older man swallowed hard. Uncomfortable, he nudged the rudder, catching the wind and causing the small vessel to pick up speed as a flock of birds rose from a field on shore.

"We're lucky to have Annie, else there's no chance we could grab a sail," Frank remarked. "Woman's a godsend, I can tell you that."

Teddy nodded. He felt a wave of guilt and balled his hands tightly. For the first time he wondered how on earth Joanna had handled all this for so long.

"It's been a terrible thing to watch," Frank said, staring off, his hand guiding the boat by instinct. "A vital woman like your mother isn't meant to lose her way, little by little, like a bird losing its feathers. It's criminal, that's all I can say . . ."

Teddy tried imagining what it must be like for his mother to see her own abilities vanishing, the ability to remember, to converse, to use a paintbrush, her capacity to express herself through her art.

As if reading his mind, the Irishman shook his head. "The worst is to see a person's passion trickle away until there's nothing there. When all this started a couple years back, I encouraged her to keep painting. To hell with the illness, I said."

Teddy looked up, surprised.

"Led her to the canvas myself, I did, every day for a week. She would stare at it for a long time and then walk away. On the last day, her hands began to shake and she backed off, a look of horror on her face." Frank grimaced at the memory. "You'd have thought she was about to harm one of her children. Once you don't trust your abilities . . . well, it's cruel is all I can say. But we can't keep her out of the studio, so there you have it."

Teddy took a beat. His mind was conjuring pieces of his family puzzle he never knew existed. "What do *you* remember about my father?" he asked.

Frank bowed his head, then took a deep breath. "He was a troubled man, your father. Always something on his mind, something preoccupying him. He would be sitting at the table having dinner with you, but he wasn't really there, he was someplace else."

Teddy nodded. He remembered trying hard to get his father's attention because he always seemed lost in thought. Demands of his job, he'd always told Teddy.

"Your mother suspected something was going on for a long time. There were rumors that she did her best to keep from you kids. Women . . ." The older man paused. "Are you sure you want to hear this?"

"Frank," Teddy said, turning to face the old man. "Who's going to tell me if you don't—my mother? Help me out here."

"He had a gal in Newton, Kate learned. The lady used to call your home in Cambridge. I wouldn't have known about this, you understand, except she called out to Sconset one summer," he said, nudging the rudder as the wind kicked up. "You must have been nine or ten. Said she was looking for Richard Mathison."

Teddy's body tightened and he looked out at the ocean.

"I'd been doing some odd jobs around the house and picked up the phone thinking it was the lumberyard. Anyway," Frank continued, his eyes carefully gauging the effect of his words, "the woman said I should inform Richard that she wouldn't be treated like a whore and that he could expect her on the five o'clock ferry that afternoon."

He rubbed his face, clearly uneasy at sharing the story. "Turns out your mother had heard it all from the phone line in the kitchen. She told me not to say anything to your father. She went herself and met that boat. Found the woman. I have no idea what she said to her, but the lady was on the next boat off the island. That was one. There were others."

Teddy looked away, shutting his eyes as a breeze kicked up. Frank studied the back of him, wanting to soften this all somehow.

"Your dad had a good heart. He was a big tipper. I once saw him stop and offer a few bucks to a crusty old fisherman down on the docks. The man had lost his boat, his livelihood, everything. Your father made a point of trying to get that man a loan, get him back on his feet." He grinned sadly. "Problem was, your father liked to spend money he didn't have."

Teddy swung around suddenly. "Hell, Frank, he was vice president of a goddamn bank. The man did all right, don't you think?"

"Apparently he lost money for the bank. Made some shaky loans that didn't pan out. He was living beyond his means, wanted everyone to think he was a big spender. His women. His family." Frank tacked toward shore, then looked at Teddy with a sad understanding. "I don't think he was a happy man, your father. He wanted to be liked and respected, but . . . well, he tried."

Teddy sat silently, filtering all of this information through a memory that had been selective for too many years. Pieces of the truth were coming together as he listened to Frank's recollections.

"The final straw for your mother, I think," Frank said gently, "was that your dad had gotten hold of the deed to your summerhouse. It belonged to her parents, you know. And he borrowed against it to pay off his debts. Nearly lost it to the bank. She worked for years after, painting like mad, selling off her work to keep the island house and your home in Cambridge. They had been in her family, you see. She'd wanted to pass them on to you and Joanna. Your mom went over the edge on that one. She couldn't bear that he'd done it. It was just after that when it happened—" Frank broke off.

Teddy looked at him, nodding with pained comprehension. "'I made your life miserable,'" he said, repeating the words from his father's suicide note.

The two remained silent for some time. Teddy scanned out to sea, the wind kicking up whitecaps in the water. Frank followed his gaze.

"Give me a break and take the rudder, would you? That's the lad," he said, shifting over.

Teddy got up and moved to the stern; grasping the tiller, he hunched down next to the older man. "Haven't done this in a long time," he warned.

Frank eyed him. "You should know that your mother put me in charge of carrying out her will," he said solemnly.

"Really," Teddy said, not all that surprised.

"Joanna knows about this, so it seems only fair to tell you. When your mum dies, the Cambridge home is to go to your sister. She stayed in Boston all these years and Kate thought it only fitting, what with you out in California most of the time."

"Sounds right." Teddy nodded, getting reacquainted with the feel of a tiller in his hand.

"The summerhouse," the Irishman added without fanfare, "is to go to you."

"What?" Teddy looked over, utterly surprised.

Frank nodded. "You were the artist, your mother insisted, even when you became a lawyer and stopped visiting. She was certain, Kate was, that you'd come someday." The older man smiled warmly. "And you have, Teddy-boy. Just the way she said you would."

Teddy was astonished at this news. Only the sound of the flapping sail broke the silence in the boat as he puzzled over this revelation.

"When they first diagnosed this disease, your mother told me she would never bear it," Frank said. "Kate had this notion that she'd simply go out for one last swim one day and that would be that. She'd give herself over to the ocean that she loved so much." He grew quiet.

Numb, Teddy shook his head slowly at the unbearable thought of his mother disappearing into the waters she had long painted and enjoyed.

"She asked me to help her carry out that wish if things got too bad, if you can believe it." Frank smiled sadly. "But I could never do a thing like that. Thank God, that wish has disappeared from her memory, along with so much else." He gazed out at several yachts and colorful sails navigating the waters ahead. The wind was shifting direction and the sail gave a shudder and sagged. "The boat's in irons," he announced, reaching over to flip the jib and bring the boat about. "Remember what that means?"

"Yeah," Teddy answered automatically. "She's lost the wind." His mind was recalling another scene. "You remember the way my mother used to race down to the beach after she'd finished a painting?" he asked Frank, his eyes fixed on the horizon. "The way she'd climb into that old boat of hers, row out a hundred yards or so, let out one hell of a holler, and dive in . . ."

Frank nodded. "Ah, the ritual," he recalled with a wink of appreciation. "The *swim of celebration,* she called it. Amazing woman, your mother.

"Even now, in her condition, she'll wander down to the water without anyone knowing. You have to keep a sharp eye out, lock the gates, that sort of thing. She's got a will of iron, that one."

Teddy sat pensively, gazing out to sea and smiling.

"Passion," the Irishman acknowledged with a sad shake of his head. "That's what she was all about. Pure passion. For art, for her children, for life itself." He paused, studying Teddy. "How about you, lad?"

"What do you mean?"

"Your work. First the law, now politics. Running for the Senate. Have you found your passion, boy?"

Teddy thought of the success he'd had in the courtroom, becoming a media darling, the perks of a high profile, the money, not to mention the women who were drawn to him. Prominence bred control and control bred power. He was a man of ambition, one who had been courted by people in high places.

Straightening, he looked into the Irishman's curious eyes. But for the life of him, Teddy didn't have an answer.

24

Teddy pulled into the parking lot of the Windswept Cranberry Bog in the late afternoon and immediately grew concerned. Not only was there no sign of Zoe, there was no sign of anyone. He double-checked his watch. Five o'clock. Right on time, as he had been every afternoon that whole week. He got out of the car feeling anxious and somehow unnerved. He must have looked that way, too.

"Didn't you read the note we sent home?" came a woman's voice.

Teddy whirled around to find Liza emerging from the trail that led off the moors. He felt the heat rising to his cheeks. He'd avoided her since the first day of classes and hated to be caught off guard. Not being ambushed was essential in both the courtroom and on the campaign trail. Now, facing Liza, he had no idea what it was he wanted to say.

"Obviously, I didn't," he said, clearing his throat uncomfortably.

"We dismissed early today. The kids have gone into town. We're putting some of their photos on display next week, after the Fourth. One of the gallery owners is teaching them about framing. It was all there in the note," Liza explained with a friendly smile.

"Uh-huh," Teddy sighed, disgruntled. "I guess Zoe forgot to share that with me."

"She got a ride into town with one of the kids. Said she told you. I take it she didn't?"

"No," Teddy said, then turned and started back for the car.

"Hey, what is your problem?" Liza called after him.

Teddy stopped. "Excuse me?" He turned around, hands on his hips, preparing himself for another one of her attacks.

"You've been avoiding me. Not even a courtesy wave when you drop off or pick up. That first day you were driving pretty strong to the hoop. Now it's like you've taken the ball home so no one can play. What happened? A woman doesn't give it up right away so you give up?"

Teddy was mystified. "Look, you turned on me like some kind of rabid dog. In front of my kid, I might add. Where do you get the nerve talking to me like this?"

"Oh, come on, you big baby," she shot back. "We both know you were coming on to me here in the parking lot. It wasn't appropriate and you didn't want to admit I was right."

"You embarrassed me."

"You deserved it," she responded, her eyes flashing.

"But in front of my daughter?"

"*Especially* in front of her," she declared, unbowed and in his face. "Hey, don't you remember? Rule number three, I think it was: 'Nothing happens in front of your teenage daughter ever!'"

"You remember that?" he said, surprised.

"Yeah," Liza mused. "At least one of us did."

Something about her not pulling any punches appealed to Teddy. And, damn it, she was as attractive as hell. He allowed a small grin. "You're pretty ferocious, you know that?"

"Yeah," she said, hands on her hips. "That's why the men are beating down my door."

Teddy scratched his head. "Could be an attitude thing. Most guys don't like someone pointing out everything they're doing wrong."

"Touché," she allowed with a nod of her head and a bare glimpse of lightheartedness. "I'll keep that in mind."

"Good," Teddy said. "Glad we got that cleared up." He hesitated, wanting to say something else to her, but he dismissed it and headed for his car.

"If you've got a few minutes," Liza called out, "there's something I think you should see."

Teddy turned and grinned. "Talk about a line," he said. "Lady, I can't figure you out."

"Been there, heard that," she bantered, gesturing for him to come along.

Curious, Teddy followed her over to the trail and onto a pathway that wound through a grove of pine and cedar. Admiring the view of the woman walking in front of him, he made a point to hold his tongue. He didn't want to get tripped up mistakenly offering a *come-on* when what he meant was a *compliment.* Suddenly, an errant branch snapped at him out of nowhere and Teddy ducked to avoid it. Popping up, slightly disoriented, he heard sly laughter coming from up ahead and shook his head. Liza seemed dedicated to keeping him off guard.

Approaching an opening, Teddy made out a small building nestled in a meadow. The squat, boxlike wooden structure had the island's typical gray-shingled surface that was offset by a long white flower box attached beneath a wide central window. A large irregular slab of rock served as the one-step stairway before the front door, and a modest sign attached above the window, hand-painted, bore the ungainly designation NATURE RESERVE CENTER AND ART GALLERY.

"This is where it all happens," Liza announced as they entered the clearing. "Well, at least when we're out in the field. Come on in." She threw on a light and directed Teddy toward the opposite corner but quickly noticed he wasn't budging. Instead, he appeared transfixed by a wall covered in a series of stunning photographs taken of the island.

"Are they yours?" Teddy asked, spellbound.

"Yes," she replied self-consciously. "But that's not why I brought you here."

"Give me a moment," he whispered. Here was Liza's own work. Teddy lost all sense of himself, allowing the images and colors to wash over him as he had when he viewed his mother's last, unfinished painting that first evening. He fixed on a photograph that captured a flock of geese rising against a brightening sky, the mood dominated by the lush reds and pinks and yellows of dawn.

Another photograph was filled with the cool blue of dazzling waters interrupted by the lone figure of a fisherman standing waist deep, his pole arching hopefully forward, a translucent moon overhead. The next photograph brought a smile to Teddy's face. It was the lighthouse next to his family's Sconset home, captured in the stark twilight, rising ghostly from the waters.

He might not know a lot about photography, but Teddy recognized in Liza's work the same effect as in his mother's paintings—the use of light was astonishing. Teddy turned to her, smiling in a way Liza had never seen before. It was soft, endearing, even sweet somehow.

"I had no idea," he said in barely a whisper.

The heat Teddy had been feeling as he followed her on the path seemed to transfer to his head. He felt flushed. The artistry of the photographs was overpowering. Something unfamiliar stirred within him, a sense, suddenly, of unworthiness. He took a step back.

"What is it?" Liza asked with a note of concern.

"It's just . . . ," Teddy stumbled. "Your photographs, they're amazing." He paused. "You see, when you talked about photography I thought maybe, all right, she snaps pictures. You know, the kind you put in a scrapbook. But this . . . ," he said, gesturing toward the wall of her work, his face clearly moved. "Liza, this is magnificent. Really. It's art."

His words moved her and she tried not to let him see how much.

"Thanks," she said softly.

Teddy felt a renewed attraction to her, only this was something deeper. Yes, she was attractive, but those photographs, that passion. He felt moved in a way he normally didn't with women. Of course, besides Judith, it had been twentysomethings who most often turned his head. But this woman in front of him was different from all of them. Everything about her seemed outside his experience. And then, instead of test-driving the line before using it, the words simply tumbled out. "I'd like to get to know you better. Could we maybe go out?"

Liza studied him for a moment. Teddy could see she was holding back. She was wrestling with something. "All right," she said guardedly. "On the condition that I get to plan our time."

Teddy was taken aback but grinned at her boldness. "I can go along with that."

They stood there for a moment in silence. And then, suddenly, Liza exclaimed, "I almost forgot the reason I brought you here!" She took him by the arm and led him to a darkened corner of the room. Flipping a switch, she directed a wall-mounted track light onto a single photograph hanging there.

Teddy's eyes moved across it carefully. It was the figure of a solitary girl amid the tall grass of a Nantucket beach. The girl reminded him of his own daughter, at half her present age. He noted the open expression on the child's face. She appeared transparent in her vulnerability: a fuller, taller, human version of the grass as it stood blowing in the breeze, starkly beautiful and utterly alone.

"Liza, it's remarkable. It's like you can see inside that little girl."

"I'd like to take credit for it. But this one's not mine," Liza said softly.

Teddy turned to her. "Whose is it?"

"It was taken by one of the best young talents I've ever come across." She paused. "This one's by Zoe."

He was visibly stunned. "Zoe? Zoe did this?"

Liza smiled and nodded happily.

Teddy turned and stared at the figure of the little girl in the photograph. Her eyes appeared to be looking back directly into his own. She seemed so small, so exposed, and yet somehow incredibly brave as she held her head up, peering straight ahead into the camera, which caught everything with perfect clarity and compassion.

"Zoe . . . ," he whispered, unable to turn away.

25

You're not going out with her. You're not going to ruin this for me," Zoe shouted from the top of the stairs.

"It's just a date," Teddy tried explaining from down in the foyer. "She's a nice person. She likes me. I like her. What's so bad about that?" He was growing anxious because he'd asked Frank to come over and cover for him and the older man was late.

"I don't want her to like you," Zoe protested. "Everything you touch in my life turns to shit."

"Zoe . . ."

"No. You don't know how to treat people," she shouted. "Face it, Dad, you're a freak."

"And you're a kid, Zoe; you don't understand how it works between grown-ups," he argued, shooting a glance at his watch.

"Are you for real?" she retorted. "You fall madly in love, you make a baby, then you split, isn't that how it goes?"

Teddy tried taking a deep breath. It didn't help. It was the last day of June and Judith was now phoning and e-mailing practically every five minutes. She carried on about being turned into a laughingstock in the eyes of her high-powered colleagues, who taunted her for running a campaign with *no* candidate! She pointed out that little more than a week remained until the debate, slightly over six weeks until the special election. On top of it, Teddy had missed the appearance before the party heads. He was to have attended that event in person and was forced to conference in his remarks two evenings prior. Of course, the power brokers had all paid lip service to the importance of family and congratulated him on doing the right thing.

"Sorry," Frank called out, breathless, as he burst through the door.

"Hi, Frank," he said, excited and relieved that the man had arrived. "I'm trying to explain to Zoe here that by dating her teacher I'm not trying to horn in on her turf." He took a step up the stairs toward his daughter. "I don't want to make things uncomfortable for you . . ."

"Good. Then cancel the date," Zoe said, staring back as if she would breathe fire if she could.

Teddy brightened. "Hey, Liza showed me that photo you took of the young girl. The one in the tall grass?"

"She what?" Zoe sputtered.

"Your photo, it's incredible." Teddy grinned. "You have to see it, Frank," he said, turning back to enlist the Irishman in his cause.

"I'd really like to—" Frank started.

"She had no right to show it to you," Zoe objected, pounding her fist against the wall. "I didn't want you to see it."

"Why not? She's proud of you and the photograph. It's amazing, Zoe."

"Because," Zoe roared down the stairs, "it's private. It's mine!" The sound of her door slamming reverberated through the house.

Teddy's eyes remained on the top of the stairs.

"I don't get it," he said, shaking his head. "I can't win with her."

"You were her age once," Frank said as he unhooked a couple of fish he'd hauled in for lunch and walked toward the kitchen to prepare them. "And you were no picnic, I can tell you that," he called over his shoulder.

Turning back, Teddy saw that his mother had entered the foyer. Kate was gazing up at him, a seeming sadness filling her features. Seeing her unexpectedly reminded Teddy of how he himself had rebelled against her in much the same way as Zoe, raging and storming off on many occasions. He had been exactly Zoe's age when his rebellion took shape. Shutting his eyes, he ground his teeth in frustration. Thank God he was heading out with Liza, he told himself. Everything in his life, this family, was so overwhelming. He needed the respite. His mother's expression seemed suddenly wise and knowing.

"I'm late," he muttered and hurried out.

26

Liza had asked Teddy to meet her at the Wauwinet Hotel. The Topper Room there was known for its sumptuous weekend brunches, and he was looking forward to dining out on the deck. But when he arrived, dressed casually elegant in tan pants, white shirt, and navy blue blazer, he found Liza waiting for him in the parking lot. To his surprise she was wearing a dazzling evergreen bikini.

"I think you might raise a few eyebrows dining in that," Teddy deadpanned. "But you won't get an argument from me."

"We're not having brunch," she said, giving him a sly smile. "We need a little physical outlet first. You're entirely too uptight," she teased. "Go on, you'll need these." She held out a pair of men's trunks.

"Liza, look," Teddy protested, "if you want to go for a swim . . ."

"Who said anything about swimming?" she replied brightly.

Liza stood as lookout while Teddy changed in the car. She then led him down to the harbor. A motorboat and driver were waiting to take them out to sea. Teddy looked at the contraption mounted on the boat and froze in horror.

"What's that?" he asked, eyeing the apparatus nervously.

Liza grinned. "I thought so." She nodded like a doctor confirming her diagnosis. "You've never been parasailing."

"No," Teddy stammered. "Look," he said, turning to her, his eyes betraying the fear he was feeling. "I'm not really good with heights. Flying is tough for me."

"Cheer up." Liza smiled. "I'll be there with you and there's absolutely nothing that can happen that you can't get out of. I promise."

Teddy's ego got the better of him and he did his best to look nonchalant. Moments later, he found himself being strapped into a tandem harness. Before he could think of a graceful way out, the two of them were riding out to sea with the boat's driver. Teddy stared up at the open sky, his heart racing with trepidation.

As he tried wrapping his mind around how he'd allowed himself to be put in this position, Teddy felt a pull on the tether and he and Liza were being launched from the powerboat. The line was given slack, the sail above their tandem harness began to lift, and together Liza and Teddy rose into the air.

His face white with fear, Teddy turned to his copilot and, voice shaking, stated the obvious. "You're not like other women I've met."

Liza grinned. "Good." Letting out a holler of delight, she pointed skyward and, over Teddy's protests, the boat driver let the line go, sending them swooping up into the air, turning them into human kites.

Gliding along, Teddy held tight to the harness. He could hear Liza's squeals of laughter but didn't dare look at her. Only when he felt her hand clasping down on his did he muster the courage to steal a glance. She was throwing her head back with unbridled joy and the sight of her calmed him a bit.

"Isn't this the *greatest*?" she called out.

Teddy smiled weakly. It took him several more minutes before he dared to take a peek around. He nervously peered down at the boat to which they were attached and then up at the boldly colored parachute above their heads. Settling down slightly, he was finally able to scan the scene around and below him. He found an unobstructed view of the ocean and coastline that was breathtaking, as if he could now for the first time see the broad brushstrokes of nature on the earth's canvas. Swallowing hard, he stared down at the water running swiftly beneath him. It was as if he and Liza had sprouted wings.

For a few minutes, his lack of control over the contraption they were riding caused him to panic again. Glancing over at Liza, he could see how she had given herself over to the feeling with abandon.

"Let go, Teddy," she roared. "Just ride it. Whoa!" she shouted as the wind lifted them even higher.

Teddy did his best to follow suit, leaning back in the harness ever so slightly. As he did he caught sight of the magnificent sky above and ahead of them. It was brilliantly blue, and as he gazed at it, a chill of recognition shot up his spine. "Bluer than blue," he whispered with awe. And with that, he gave himself over, letting out a holler that surprised him and delighted his parasailing partner.

The two rode on, exchanging excited glances. The touch of her hand a hundred feet above the ground was electric. He was alive with the thrill of the unexpected. Later, as the driver reeled them in, Teddy felt, coursing through his body, the nervous excitement of a child who's just been taken on the wildest roller-coaster ride in the park.

"Wow. I feel completely out of control and I'm okay," he shouted over at Liza. "It's amazing."

She grinned and nodded enthusiastically. "Control is entirely overrated, don't you think?" She laughed.

Once they were safely back on board the boat, the driver helped the two of them out of their harnesses. Teddy was surprised at the momentary disappointment he felt, as if someone had taken away his privileges. He looked up and found Liza smiling at him.

"Hungry?" she asked.

"Starved." He grinned.

Shortly thereafter, they sat on the outside deck of the Wauwinet, downing seafood and beer. Liza had changed into soft red shorts and a matching pullover. It looked comfortable and sexy to Teddy. He watched in amazement as Liza moaned, dipping lobster in butter and sliding it seductively past her lips. This wasn't a meal—it was foreplay. He chuckled to himself, because no woman he knew in California would be caught dead stuffing her face with wild abandon. And certainly not while on a date. She might order a salad and pick at it throughout the meal. Seeing Liza make love to her food was both sensuous and refreshing. They chatted about everything under the sun with the ease of old friends, and Teddy felt lighter than he had in years.

When the subject of his campaign came up, Liza couldn't help getting in a dig. "Uh-oh." She smiled. "Dating a waitress. That's sure to go over big with the people funding your campaign."

Teddy flashed on Judith. Liza was right. He could just imagine the disapproval. Not out of jealousy. Their sex, as his high-powered campaign manager often liked to point out, was nothing more than a mutual arrangement. No, Judith would go nuclear because dating Liza couldn't possibly do anything for his family values or any other polling numbers she could think of. He didn't care and quickly shook it off.

"I'd like to meet your mom," Liza said.

"Man, you island women move quickly." Teddy laughed.

"No, no, it's just . . ." Liza shook her head, growing serious. "I really am an admirer."

"I see. Just using me to get to my mother," he teased. Yet, for some reason that he couldn't put his finger on, Teddy knew right then that he wanted Liza to meet Kate as well. Again, he found himself wishing, even for the slightest of moments, that his mother could be the woman and the artist she once had been.

27

Teddy checked his rearview mirror to make sure Liza was right behind him. He'd asked her to come back to the house with him so he could show her the old place.

His cell went off and he answered it.

"Bad news," came Judith's power voice. "Got a call from Sacramento. The party movers have decided to look more closely at the other candidates. You need to wrap things up and get back here tomorrow. Do you hear me, Teddy?"

"What are you talking about?" He laughed, a bit giddy. "The governor himself called me a slam dunk."

"Really," she replied curtly. "Maybe you haven't heard of a little thing called 'out of sight, out of mind.'"

"Come on, Judith. You can handle this. Put out some good copy. I'll wrap things up as fast as I can. Promise."

There was a pause. "You know, all this can't be about your mother, Teddy. Christ," she said, "have you gone and met someone?"

"What are you talking about?" Teddy asked, sounding genuinely puzzled. "I'm taking care of my mother, Judith. Get me a few radio interviews I can do from here. That'll shut up the fat cats." He grinned.

"Party primaries are a funny animal, Teddy," Judith replied pointedly. "People pick up on something, get a bad feeling, who knows why the hell they get skittish. I suggest you get your ass back here now. And bring me my photograph!" The line went dead.

"Oh, shit!" Teddy muttered, banging his hand softly on the steering wheel. He knew she was right, but he really didn't care. Then he remembered Judith's remark that he was not the relationship type. Not true, he told himself. And then he rounded the bend and the sight of Frank's worried face as he pulled into the driveway pierced what was left of the high he'd been feeling.

"What's happened, Frank?" he called out as Liza drove up behind him and stepped out of her old VW. She walked up to Teddy as he got out of his car.

"I couldn't stop her, Teddy, I'm sorry. I tried to reach you on your cell phone but I got your machine and I hung up."

"Frank, just . . ."

"I couldn't leave Kate here alone or I would have gone after her—" he protested.

Teddy cut him off. "What is it?"

"Zoe left in a state," the Irishman said, clearly shaken. "She was all worked up . . . something about you going out with her teacher," Frank said, glancing at Liza, who stood solemnly next to Teddy as the older man delivered the news. "She didn't want to listen to me."

"She couldn't have gone very far on foot, even using the bicycle . . . ," Teddy thought out loud.

"That's just it," Frank said. "She called some boy she said was from her photography group. He pulled up on a motorbike and the two of them drove off."

"Motorbike." Teddy's brow creased with worry. He turned to Liza. "Do you know anything about this kid?"

"I think I have some idea." She nodded. "There's a young man in the group who drives a motorbike. I've noticed him and Zoe talking quite a bit together. He's from Slovakia, here on a summer visa. Must be eighteen or nineteen, but he wanted to study photography so much I let him in."

"I told them to wait for you and then . . . ," Frank offered, trying to find the words. "Well, they just drove off."

"Listen, Teddy," Liza said, pulling him aside. "When I agreed to go out with you, I didn't think enough about what that would mean to Zoe. Kids need boundaries to be respected just like we do. You and I had a great time, but we both know rule number one when it comes to single dads and the women they date—your first responsibility is to your daughter."

"My daughter is a beautiful young woman who is in the process of pushing every boundary she can. My not seeing you isn't going to solve the problem," he said, looking into her eyes.

Liza put her hand on his. "Maybe not, but you two have some things to work out. It's important that I step back so you can have the room to do that."

He stared into her eyes with consternation.

Liza seemed to have made up her mind. She brushed her fingers through her hair absentmindedly. "I'm going to run over to the nature center in case they stopped by there," she said. "Let me know if there's anything else I can do. Please, Teddy, phone me when you find her." She gave him a hug that lingered for just a beat longer than either might have expected. "And, remember, you will find her and someday the two of you will look back on this and hug each other."

Helpless, Teddy watched her get into her car, give him a little wave, and then drive off.

"Damn it!" Teddy muttered, his mind racing.

Frank patted him on the back and turned to go inside. "I better check on Kate. Why don't you come in? Maybe Zoe will be back at any moment."

Upset and worried, Teddy followed. "What the hell's the point," he asked, moving through the house toward the art studio. "Can you tell me that, Frank? What good is caring about any of this? My mother's disappearing before my eyes, my daughter hates everything about me . . ." He gestured wildly. "I find a woman really worth knowing and she's already walking away."

Teddy entered the studio and found Frank helping his mother over to the window. His sense of powerlessness was both foreign and overwhelming.

"You hear this, Kate?" he called out as he paced. "Zoe's run off with some boy just to spite me. She wants nothing to do with me, wants to get as far away from me as possible."

He paused, his eyes on Kate. It struck him that this was all some divine retribution for everything he'd done to his mother. More than anyone, he supposed, she would know exactly what it feels like to have a child run from you.

"What would you do, Mom?" he asked her, as if somehow he could *will* her to give him parental advice.

As she had days ago in that studio, Kate turned to him, locking her eyes on his. "Never give up on who or what you love!"

Teddy held her gaze a moment and it was a moment that suddenly moved him to tears. He nodded. She was lucid and she was right. He impulsively kissed her forehead. Turning, Teddy sprinted through the house and out to his car.

28

After racing into town, Teddy parked in the lot at Straight Wharf and searched the bustling pier, but he came up empty. He got back in his car and drove through Main Street and several offshoots to no avail. Trying to think like a teenage boy, Teddy shot over to Cisco Beach, his eyes scanning the roads for a motorbike, wanting desperately to find Zoe and, at the same time, flinching at the thought of spotting her with her arms wrapped around some strange guy as they navigated the road.

He drove to Ram's Pasture, got out, and jogged along its open land, his eyes managing to ferret out the bushes where his daughter and this boy could be hidden, God forbid, doing what he didn't want to imagine. His search turned up no sign of her, and he moved on to the tall reeds of Hummock Pond, to Great Point, where kids were flying kites and where he managed to spot a couple rolling in the grass. He got more than an earful when he sprang on them without warning. Growing more frustrated, Teddy doubled back to Altar Rock in the moors, having to make the last bit of the trek on foot due to the sandy roads. No Zoe. As he headed for the beach at Surfside, his cell rang. It was Liza.

"She's not at the center," she reported. "Have you tried Jetties Beach? There's some event there today. A DJ playing music. It's a big teen hangout. I'd head over but I think Zoe may not want to see me right now."

"Sure, makes sense," Teddy agreed.

"I'm sorry, Teddy. If there's anything I can do . . ."

Teddy held the wheel tightly. "Thanks," he said. "I'll let you know when I find her." He flipped the phone off. He could feel the opening he had experienced with Liza slamming shut. It was hard to believe how different things had been a mere two hours earlier—in the air above the island, Liza beside him. As he turned the car around, it occurred to Teddy that Liza had it only half right. Zoe might not want to see her right now, but she most definitely didn't want to see her father.

Teddy made it into the parking lot at Jetties Beach not far from the lighthouse at Brant Point. It seemed as if the whole island was there—kids, parents; it was a maelstrom of activity. Scanning the lot, Teddy found a number of motorcycles and scooters in addition to cars and bicycles. He ran out onto the beach and was hit by a wave of rock music blaring from speakers mounted on a makeshift stage. There were so many kids he hardly knew where to start. He circled the crowd and found a number of girls decked out in skimpy outfits, not one of them dressed like Zoe would be. Pushing through the multitudes, his eyes darted from teen to teen gyrating in the sand, dancing, making out.

Emerging from the crowd, Teddy headed for the water's edge. His mind flashed on the little girl who loved running along the beach in Malibu. And then, as he walked around a sand dune, Teddy's heart leapt into his throat. A tall, muscular young man was leaning over his daughter. He had her pinned against a storm fence and she did not look comfortable. Teddy could see the look of concern on his daughter's face, as if she were in over her head and suddenly remembered that she couldn't swim.

Teddy raced up the sandy slope and, taking the kid by surprise, pulled him off of Zoe and sent him crashing to the ground.

"What's the problem?" the young man shouted in a foreign accent. "Who do you think you are?" He rose to his feet, ready for a fight.

Zoe registered relief momentarily, before turning on her father. "What are you doing here?" she asked, looking a little odd in a long-sleeved shirt and jeans on a hot summer's day at the beach.

Teddy's eyes remained on the eighteen-year-old clenching his fists before him. "I'm her father," Teddy told him coldly. "You touch my daughter again, you're a dead man."

"This is your father?" the boy asked Zoe.

She nodded, biting her lip nervously.

"She's thirteen. You know what the penalties are for statutory rape? You could be in jail for a *long* time."

The young man took a step backward. He shot a look at Zoe, then turned and sprinted away.

Teddy glanced at the spectators who'd gathered nearby, then back at his daughter.

"Oh my God, what are you *doing* here?" she yelled.

"That's the way you thank me?" he asked, looking genuinely confused. "I just saved you from young Arnold Schwarzenegger over there and this is what you say to me?"

"I don't need you to save me," Zoe spat back, yet her face looked relieved through her false bravado.

"The guy is five years older than you, Zoe. You're still a kid!" Teddy countered, growing red in the face as a small crowd continued to gather around them.

"Hypocrite!" she shouted. "You run around dating women half your age, you *perv*."

Teddy's eyes darted among the beach crowd gazing back at him. He had told Miranda it would be a disaster to bring Zoe with him to the island and he had been right. The hurt and anger between them was so immense that neither seemed capable or willing to move beyond it.

"Hey, aren't you running in the California primary?" came a disembodied voice off to his right.

Teddy pivoted to find a tanned, middle-aged man standing a few yards away with his wife.

"Sure, sure. I know you," the man continued excitedly. "I've seen you on television. Teddy Mathison, right?"

Teddy's mouth went dry, his face drained of color.

"We're the Andersons from San Diego. Come to Nantucket every summer," the man went on exuberantly. "Well, look at this, a fellow island aficionado. We heard you were dropping out of the race, that so?"

Teddy winced at the suggestion. "No, absolutely not," he

said, trying to absorb this news while wondering where the guy had heard a thing like that.

The man grinned. "Well, guess who we'll be voting for, hey, Marcy?" he bellowed, smiling at his blond wife, who was standing quietly beside him.

"Why, thank you very much. Nice to meet you two," Teddy said with a wide grin, making a move to leave with Zoe, who had pulled back the minute her father was recognized.

"Would this be your daughter?" the man asked cheerfully. "Gosh, you must be proud of your dad."

Teddy swallowed hard as Zoe stared back at the man, her face a blank.

The man and his wife looked at Teddy and laughed uncomfortably as Zoe walked toward the parking lot.

"My daughter isn't very happy with me just now." Teddy shrugged. "You two have a nice day," he said with a forced grin, shaking their hands and following Zoe.

As they made their way to the car, Teddy could make out the strains of "Satisfaction" by the Rolling Stones wafting from the loudspeakers as an animated DJ whipped up the crowd. "I can't get no, satisfaction, no, no, no," Mick Jagger belted.

"I know what you mean, Mick," Teddy muttered, running his hand through his hair as Zoe stalked ahead of him. "I know what you mean . . ."

29

The drive was spent in tense silence. The minute they got home Zoe bolted past Frank, nearly knocking the older man over, as she ran from her father.

"Well, things look pretty much the way they were," he told Teddy, shaking his head. "How'd the boy look when you got through with him?"

"Oh, he got off easy. I just threatened to kill him," Teddy said, clasping Frank's shoulder. The sun was setting and he was tired.

"Your mom's gone to bed. Couldn't keep her eyes open. Maybe you should get a little rest yourself."

"Yeah, Frank, good idea. It's been a long day. You must be tired, too. You should go home and relax. Thank you for your help today."

The older man's kindly eyes were on him as he said, "You aren't the first parent to wonder if they'll survive their child's adolescence and you won't be the last."

Teddy smiled in spite of himself and the two men hugged.

Watching Frank drive off, Teddy remained on the steps, quietly taking in the nightfall. He had promised to phone Liza when he found Zoe, and he would as soon as he poured himself a little scotch.

The phone rang and he jumped. He looked to see who it was and reluctantly answered it.

"About time. I've been trying to get through to you for an hour," Judith said curtly, snapping Teddy back to a whole other reality.

"I'm kind of busy, Judith." Teddy pressed a finger on the throbbing vein at his temple.

"Funny, that's why I'm calling, you asshole. Don't you listen to your messages, check your e-mail, anything?"

The weary sarcasm in his campaign manager's voice was enough to make Teddy shut his eyes and lean back against the stone step.

"The party leaders are pulling the plug, Teddy. They're dropping their support for your candidacy."

"Wait a minute, Judith, this is a life-and-death situation." Teddy reacted as the words sank in. "You've got to tell them that I'm losing my mother—"

She cut him off. "What do you want from me? They say you're disengaged and they can't risk losing. You're fucking AWOL, Teddy. I've got nothing to work with. The debate is a week away. Either you get your ass back here and keep them from throwing their weight behind Hoyt or Emerson or this campaign is folding."

"Fold . . ." Teddy's heart quickened. All of his hard work, the years he'd spent building his reputation, his dreams of the Senate, his nurturing ties with the party, it was all headed south. He began to panic. What was he *doing* on Nantucket, anyway? If anything, his life had taken a turn for the worse since he'd arrived. He'd discovered the terrible secret about his father's death, but there was nothing he could do to alter the past. His mother's condition made communication difficult at best and he felt helpless watching her slip away. His mind raced. No, he needed to be doing something that could make a difference. He had too much invested in his political candidacy. Teddy's mind reeled from the roller-coaster ride he'd been on.

"Don't worry, Judith. I'm coming home," he answered firmly and flipped his cell phone closed.

The cold realization that it was the right move settled over him. Teddy was going to go home and win that primary. Nothing, not his mother, his daughter, or a brief encounter with a woman he felt oddly attached to, was going to derail that.

It was time to take back his life.

30

After phoning Liza and leaving a message that he had found Zoe and she was okay, Teddy made his way up the stairs to pack. He realized only now that he must have sounded curt to a woman he had true feelings for. He promised himself he would phone and leave a nicer message when he got back to L.A. Maybe he'd come back for another visit when things settled down and they could try to pick up where they left off.

Reaching the top of the stairs, Teddy saw Zoe's closed door and shook his head. He headed for his room but instead was drawn farther down the hallway to look in on his mother. He gently pushed the door open and peered in. It was already evening but he could see Kate clearly with the light from a full moon pouring in the window. Her breathing was labored as he stepped in for a closer look. Despite the harsh rasping noise she emitted, Teddy noted the serene look on her face as she slept. He studied her wrinkled skin, the softness of her features, the way her hair splayed out over the pillow. He took a deep breath and let it out slowly.

It occurred to him that with his determination to leave the island the next day, this might well be the last time he would see his mother. He felt suddenly fragile, rubbing his forehead at the finality of it all. Still, looking down at her again, he knew what she would do if she were in his position. Life had to go on. He needed to take Zoe back home and return to his responsibilities. His mother, of all people, would understand that. He reached out and stroked her hand. Then, pushing a strand of hair away from her face, Teddy sadly turned and left the room.

His heart was heavy, but he was nevertheless resolute. He knew what he needed to do. As he made his way down the hall he realized it would be better to tell Zoe of his decision tonight rather than spring it on her in the morning. He was concerned she might already be asleep, so he didn't knock. He simply opened Zoe's door very quietly and looked in. She was on the bed, hunched over intently. His eyes took her in, but his brain had trouble registering what she was doing. And then he froze.

Zoe sat on the edge of the bed, earphones in place, her left arm dripping blood. Teddy blinked, unable to comprehend what he was witnessing. God. No. His little girl was *mutilating* herself.

The blood pounded in his ears, the world kicked out from under him. In horror, Teddy gazed at the scarlet lines on his daughter's arm, self-inflicted wounds that had been torn in pain and scarred over and torn again.

"Zoe . . . ," he gasped, his voice deep and frightened, but she didn't seem to hear him. "Zoe!" he cried out, the agony of this reality settling in.

She looked up and screamed, "Get out!"

Teddy's synapses were firing in slow motion. His feet felt as if they were encased in concrete as he stared wild-eyed at the sharp metal instrument in his daughter's hand, his eyes focusing on the blood smeared on the scissor blades. There was a flash as she waved him away, and now he was peering at her left arm, her skin reddened, blood oozing from a fresh wound, thin red scars torn in her flesh. And as his mind soaked in each image, the agonizing reality of Zoe's suffering slammed into Teddy's brain, detonating there like a grenade on impact.

Teddy stared at his daughter's face, suddenly seeing the full extent of the pain within her. This was the daughter he had always loved beyond measure and she was hurt beyond his imagining. It tore at him and humbled him.

With his heart thundering, Teddy moved forward and put his arms around Zoe, silently removing the sharp instrument from her hand. She screamed in anguish for him to let her go, she beat at him with her fists, wild and wounded like a captured animal, but he simply gathered her to his chest and held on. And then, for once in his life, propelled by a force outside of himself, he did something right.

"I'm so sorry, Zoe . . ." The words tumbled out of him as he began rocking her back and forth as he once had when she was a child. "I didn't know you were in so much pain."

After several minutes, he felt her weaken, her body growing limp until the fight drained out of her. Teddy could feel her heart against his. She was silent for a second, and then she broke into a primal, heartrending wail, sobbing into her father's chest.

She cried without ceasing as Teddy continued to rock her gently, his own eyes brimming with tears as he touched his face to the top of her head. Her body was shaking, her cry for help growing more frenzied in pitch as it climbed out of her. And then, when the fullness of her tears had been spent, she lay weakly against him as Teddy continued to stroke her hair and soothe her.

Teddy was aware of how the word "sorry" kept pouring from his lips. It reminded him of his own father, drunk on the beach, looking up at him and repeating the word, lost and afraid. Teddy, too, felt lost and afraid, but he stopped repeating the word. It disgusted him now. It meant nothing. Looking down, he gently touched his daughter's left arm with its thin red scars and the newest cut she had just made.

"My little girl." He softly wept, running his fingers lovingly across her arm. "My sweet, sweet Zoe . . ."

Zoe stared out through her tears. She had no energy left. She was numb.

Trembling, Teddy was seized with a fierce protectiveness; he held her to him, suddenly realizing that nothing more precious existed than this girl, this young woman.

31

Teddy stayed with Zoe through the evening, first tending to the fresh wound on her arm and then sitting by her bedside, brushing the hair from her eyes and telling her stories from her childhood. And then, mercifully, she drifted off to sleep.

Later, splashing water on his face in the bathroom, he thought of Miranda. He was certain she hadn't a clue what was going on with their daughter either—if she'd known she would have been the first to blame him. He stared up at himself in the mirror, considering. He wasn't to blame. He couldn't be to blame, he told himself. Lots of kids go through divorces. They don't start mutilating themselves. Why would Zoe do it?

His mind struggled to process it. That's why she always wore long-sleeved shirts and sweaters in the middle of summer. Teddy thought about how long this must have been going on—months, more than a year? He had no idea.

He stopped cold, eyeing himself again closely. That was it. He had *no idea*. He could answer reporters' questions in detail, tell you about the other candidates—their positions on welfare or the U.S.-Mexico border, who they cheated on, how much they spent on their clothes—but he had no clue as to when his own daughter had begun cutting herself.

Teddy's brain was reeling. The thought "How could she?" popped into his mind and his conscience answered harshly. *Don't you dare blame that little girl. What did she ever do to you but try to love you, ask you to spend some time with her rather than buy her off?* Teddy looked hard at himself and the only image he saw was that of a monster.

Taking the stairs to the roof two at a time, Teddy paced the widow's walk and allowed the evening wind off the ocean to calm him. Folding his arms against the rail, he leaned out, scanning the dark waters, feeling utterly ashamed and alone.

Without thinking, he pulled his cell phone from his pocket and dialed a number.

"Liza," he began. "I don't even know why I'm calling," he said, his voice heavy with emotion.

"What's wrong, Teddy?"

Teddy hesitated, wanting nothing more than to let her throw him a lifeline. But he didn't do relationships, he reminded himself. He'd just screw up one more life in the process. No. This was his problem to deal with, he knew. He had no business involving someone else.

"I'm sorry. I shouldn't have called. Just pretend this didn't happen. I've got to go," he said softly.

"All right," Liza responded, her voice full of concern.

She listened for a moment. He didn't hang up. "Teddy?" she said, sensing the pain in him. "Whatever it is, you don't have to be alone."

"Thank you," he said quietly.

Teddy put the phone away and turned to face the stairs. At that moment he had an instinct he hadn't felt in nearly thirty years. It was the need to reach out to the person he had no risk of hurting. She'd told him long ago that a mother's love was unconditional, that it was there no matter what.

He hadn't believed it then. He needed to now.

32

Teddy sat near the open window, leaning forward, close to where his mother lay sleeping. Lost in memory, he listened for a few minutes to the sound of the ocean waves breaking outside in the Nantucket night.

"When she was little, Zoe used to have this habit of parroting everything I said, while still giving it her own special twist, you know?" he remembered sadly, his voice low. "Especially when I was upset with her." A smile flitted across his face, then vanished. "'Go to bed,' I'd tell her. 'Go to bed, Daddy,' she'd say. 'Children shouldn't talk back to their parents,' I'd insist. 'Parents shouldn't talk back to their kids,' she'd counter. I thought then that she had the makings of an amazing trial attorney." His voice was wistful. "She never would back down."

He placed a hand on the bed, reaching for the comfort of his mother's physical presence.

"Zoe was her own person, even at five. Always saw things in her own unique way. She was stubborn. Like you." He nodded toward his mother. "And me." He shook his head. "But what I didn't get was that she had the soul of an artist."

Teddy stared into his mother's still handsome face. Her sleep appeared troubled, her eyelids jumping as if some odd race were taking place in her mind and she was struggling to keep up.

"Of course, that comes from you, Mom," he said quietly. "You know that? The artist in her comes from you." He stared up at a photo on the wall nearest him. It was of Kate, Joanna, and himself taken at his high school graduation. He stood in the middle, sand-wiched between the two women. They were smiling. He wasn't.

"Zoe's an astounding photographer. Liza thinks so . . ." He paused. "I've made so many mistakes. What about you? How did you deal with mistakes, Mom?" He wished she would just sit up in bed and say something. "Please, would you wake up and answer me? You see, I know I haven't asked in a long, long time, but—" His voice broke off. "I need you."

Teddy smiled mournfully as he heard himself say that. "She was right," he said. "I could never be a good father because I turned my back on being your son."

His heart was in his words as they spilled out. "And now, Mom, my little girl . . . my Zoe," he struggled, "has been carv-ing these—these lines on her arm." He looked down at her. "The thing is, I never knew . . ." His voice caught in his throat. "You should see these lines, the scars. They look angry and red-der than red."

Teddy placed his face against the side of the mattress, help-less, alone. After a moment a hand began to stroke the hair on his head.

"It'll be all right, Teddy. You are a good man and you will rise to the occasion."

He slowly lifted his head. His mother was awake, her eyes focused.

"Are you back?" he asked quietly, in awe. "Is it you?"

"Of course. For the moment," she said softly, as if she were willing herself to be there for him. Her eyes concentrated hard on his. "I . . . haven't told you, Teddy . . . ," she whispered.

"Told me what?" Teddy asked, opening his eyes wider, waiting for another undisclosed fact that would change his life forever.

"That I love you." She reached out for his hand. He took hers. "That I have missed you. That you make me so proud."

She had come back to tell him what he most needed to hear on this bleak night. It was as if she knew. Teddy leaned over and kissed her forehead and said, "These are all things I would say to you, too, Mom. I love you. And I have missed you. You make me so proud."

She smiled, squeezed his hand, and closed her eyes.

33

Near midnight Teddy pulled himself together and went downstairs to put in an emergency call to Zoe's therapist in Los Angeles. The psychologist called back shortly thereafter. They talked for a long while. The woman explained how some teens turn to cutting as a way of making visible the pain they feel inside. Teddy told her that Zoe had been doing so well, discovering her talent for photography. All of this had thrown him and he was deeply alarmed.

"There might be a silver lining in all this, believe it or not," the psychologist offered. "Your discovering her secret might just allow her to begin to turn a corner. Watch her," the woman said sympathetically. "See if Zoe withdraws, stays in her room, or if she goes back into the world, back to her photography."

The therapist promised to e-mail some material on cutting, and Teddy assured her Zoe would resume therapy when they returned to Los Angeles.

As expected, Teddy's phone call to Miranda brought on accusations and recriminations as she lashed out at him, then burst into tears. She wanted to fly to Nantucket right away, but Teddy asked her not to. He told her he had contacted Zoe's therapist and shared with Miranda what the psychologist had told him. He made a promise to call her with daily updates. Liza had mentioned an upcoming photography show for the teens. Teddy suggested that it might be a good thing not to deny Zoe this opportunity to feel good about herself.

"She's going to be okay, Miranda," Teddy assured his ex-wife. "I know I've broken a lot of promises to her, and to you, but I'm not going to break this one."

Miranda said she wanted to believe him and that she'd be in touch with Zoe's therapist herself the next day. Still in tears, she hung up.

Despite being exhausted and drained, Teddy sat up the rest of the night in a chair in his mother's room, a profound sense of clarity enveloping him. Witnessing his daughter's pain had brought into bold relief the fact that he was a fraud masquerading as a success. He had controlled his image during his political campaign, but to what end? He had managed to orphan himself, leaving his daughter without a real father, his mother without a real son. The pain of that failure seemed to be more than he could bear.

He stared at his mother and shook his head at the irony of it all. It seemed to him now that he had been the one lost in a fog all these years. Had he been a better son, he might be a better father. There was nothing he could do about the past. That he knew. He could only make a difference in the present. The hours passed and he lost all track of time.

Groggy from lack of sleep, Teddy heard a noise and turned his head. He was startled to find Zoe in the doorway, freshly showered and dressed. He hadn't even realized it was already morning.

"Frank's here. He said he'd take me to class," she nearly whispered, biting her lip. "You don't look so good. Anyway, bye."

She appeared to him much like the girl in the photograph Liza had shown him—alone, vulnerable, yet brave. Slowly, she turned, but he stopped her.

"Zoe, I am so proud to have a daughter like you. Have a good day at class, and I'll be there to pick you up when it's over."

She stared at him with her mouth forming a little O.

"Okay, Daddy. See you then."

She was going back to class. Liza would be good for her. Being involved with art would be good for her. Calmed by that thought, Teddy finally put his head down.

He didn't know how long he had been asleep, but when Teddy looked up he found his mother was gone. In a stupor, needing caffeine, Teddy made his way down to the art studio. Kate was there alone, sitting in front of her unfinished painting.

"It's about time you got up," Annie chirped, crossing into the room. "Shame on you for letting your mother find her way down here all by herself. I'll just finish up a few things and come and take her for a bath," she said, picking up the tray of tea and toast she had brought out to Kate earlier. "And we mustn't let her continue to stare at this painting. It only upsets her. Please stop putting it back out."

"But I didn't . . . ," he countered weakly as Annie left the room.

Rubbing his face, Teddy started toward the easel to remove the painting as Annie had ordered. There was a bitter taste in his mouth and his body felt as if it had shut down. He took hold of the painting and was pulling it off the easel when he became aware of the intensity in his mother's eyes. They were trained laserlike on the painting in his hand. Teddy had seen such concentration on this painting before but it had never registered. He found himself studying her face now, wondering why she couldn't let go. Gazing closely at her, it unnerved him that this figure of absolute passion and creativity was afloat on a raft of incoherence. She had no control over anything, something he himself could now understand. But worse—she wasn't being allowed to try.

Teddy was suddenly overcome with the utter injustice of it all. Was this right? Was Kate truly meant to exist in this cloud until her body and what was left of her mind just gave out? He thought back to the incident when Frank had phoned him in a panic and he had returned to find his mother in a wild state, attempting to paint her unfinished canvas. There was a twinge of shame as Teddy recalled his gruesome behavior that day. He had taunted her then, urging her to apply the paint, not so she could create, but because he didn't care if she destroyed her work.

Running the episode through his head, Teddy did his best to reason it out. That incident when she had painted her arms, when she had seemed ready to create and return to her art, what if it meant that a part of her was capable of being creative? What if an island existed within the sea of her Alzheimer's where she knew *who* she was and *what* she was meant to be doing? An impulse to stay connected to her passion, to life? Frank and Annie, not to mention the medical professionals, all seemed content to simply keep his mother comfortable. But were they treating her with dignity? Above all, they sought to ensure that she was not upset or aroused in any way. She was treading water, marking time, Teddy thought. But seeing her there in her chair, he had the sudden notion that what they were doing was all backward. She needed to be more connected to life, not less.

Teddy reached out to help her up from the chair. "Mom, it's me, Teddy."

"Well, of course it is," Kate replied with the flash of a disoriented smile. "What . . . ," she fumbled. "What are we supposed to be doing?"

"I think you might be more comfortable over here." Teddy helped her up and guided her over to a chair in the center of the room, positioning her with her back to the window so that the light poured over her shoulder from behind.

"Why . . ." She giggled a little, as if finding herself in the middle of a puzzle she was too embarrassed to admit she couldn't figure out.

Teddy grabbed hold of an easel, a few tubes of paint, and a brush with a generous head. Setting the easel in front of her, he found an unused canvas lying against one wall and mounted it. He lowered the easel's legs so she would not have to stand and placed it directly in front of his mother. Kneeling down next to her, Teddy watched as Kate stared at the blank surface before her. Holding his breath, he waited.

Kate sat for a minute or two, blinking, lost, as if handed an object she neither recognized nor knew what on earth she was supposed to do with it. Teddy exhaled and looked away. Hey, it had been worth a try.

But when he reached for the canvas to move it out of her line of sight, Kate suddenly put out her hand to stop him. Teddy saw that her eyes were becoming more focused, slowly, as if responding to some instinct deep within her, intent on the empty canvas. She looked at it with total fascination, her expression growing more animated, a light switching on in her eyes that was not there seconds before. He drew closer, holding his breath.

"What do you see there, Kate?" he whispered hopefully in her ear.

His mother broke into a grin and spoke ever so haltingly, "So many . . . possibilities . . ."

Teddy took the brush and placed it in his mother's hand. He watched her fingers slowly curl around it, finding their once familiar position. Squeezing a few dabs of blue and green, yellow and magenta onto the palette, Teddy held it close to her. Kate glanced down at the colors, unsure what to do. She looked back at the canvas and closed her eyes. He observed her in silent fascination, his heart beating with excitement.

And then Kate opened her eyes again. She sat up in her chair, nodded once to the canvas, and then turned to the paints. Dabbing the brush into the blue, she lifted it to the canvas and, with a little gasp, began to paint.

34

The brush swept across the white surface of the canvas leaving a bold, blue arc. Kate studied it. Teddy felt a small tingle of a thrill. This was something, wasn't it? His mother painting again for the first time in God knows how long. But he was struck by the frown growing on her face. "What is it, Kate? The color is fine. Keep going," he urged.

But she kept staring at the broad, crude, childlike slash of paint she'd just applied.

"It's . . . wrong, isn't it?" she said, troubled.

Teddy quickly realized that while her abilities had waned with the illness, her eye still knew somehow what a stroke of her brush should look like. It had been explained to him by the doctor at the facility on the island, as well as by Frank and Annie, that while short-term memory was greatly diminished, long-term memories were more easily accessible. And this was what was happening. Kate was remembering the quality of her brushstroke and the way it had once appeared on a canvas.

Long ago, she had gone through a Pointillist period when her work appeared greatly influenced by Pissarro and Seurat. Teddy recalled marveling at her ability and discipline in applying hundreds of tiny dots of paint out of which were fashioned people and ocean and sunsets. She had gradually developed a style that had elements of Monet and owed something to Chagall—graceful bursts of color, the world as a dream. She painted ethereal fish, silver and red, yellow and orange, arching out of the water, paying homage to a translucent moon.

Each of her works required a finesse of brushwork. She employed lyrical flourishes and keen detail. Now Kate was staring at the big, sloppy swipe of her thick brush and it looked out of place. Teddy understood this and knew it must be painful somewhere inside her where her pride and craft lay. But what was the alternative?

"It's good, Kate," he coaxed. "It's big and beautiful. Here," he said, offering her the palette, "try another color. Go on. It's all right."

She hesitated, still disturbed by what she had put on the canvas. But urged on, she dipped her brush into the yellow and bisected her blue arc with a zigzag, lemony tail.

"That's it, Kate. Good, good," Teddy called out in a flush of encouragement, like a parent urging on a child to express herself for the first time.

The old woman laughed and rocked in the chair a moment, tickled by what she had done. Then, as she pulled and tugged violently to get her sweater off, she reached for the dabs of color on the palette and rubbed her bare arm in them.

"No, no, no," Teddy said, a little troubled by the mess she was making, eyeing the door, waiting for the sergeant at arms to burst through it and reprimand him. But as he grabbed hold of a rag and turned to try to wipe the paint off his mother's arm, Kate pulled it from him with comical authority.

"Don't . . . ," she said, her words drifting off as Teddy watched the way she now utilized her arm as a palette. It was too hard for her to hold the paints, he surmised, and she was making do the way she could. She was, in her own way, managing more of the process.

Teddy stood, mesmerized, as his mother began mixing paint, applying bold patches of color, squiggly lines, piling them on top of each other. She was painting. He grinned. Alive in her art.

Outside, unbeknownst to Teddy, Frank stood at the window, unable to move away from the scene he had come upon. The sight of Kate painting again was as wondrous as snow in July. And seeing her long-estranged son, almost unrecognizable when he'd arrived on island, actually making it happen, cheering her on, startled the old man.

Teddy turned back to get a few more brushes and caught sight of Frank, his face pressed to the glass, eyes filled with wonder. The two stared at one another for a moment—Teddy imagining what Frank made of this, and Frank embarrassed that he was caught observing an intensely private moment. The Irishman nodded approval, turned, and slipped away.

Teddy watched him go, took a deep breath, grabbed the brushes, and came back to find his mother throwing hers down. Her arms were covered in paint and he watched intently as she carefully placed her hand onto the canvas, right in the middle of the blue arc and yellow zigzag. Teddy knelt down next to her, the two staring together at her red-green-yellow-blue handprint.

Kate turned to her son and grinned. "Me," she whispered.

Teddy nodded solemnly. "You," he softly replied.

35

Zoe appreciated that Liza did not ask any questions when she returned to class the day after running off. Instead, her mentor was giving her room as Zoe threw herself into her photographs. Yet she couldn't help but notice that something was different with her teacher. Liza was quieter. Not purposely distant, but less effusive, detached somehow. Still, Zoe didn't dare ask what it was. The next day, however, when the last of the students had left at the end of class, Liza approached the table where Zoe was sitting, separating out her newly printed photographs.

"Zoe," she said softly as she scanned the photos scattered before her, "I just wanted to say how incredible your work is."

"Thanks," Zoe said and kept on working, waiting for some mention of the way she'd reacted to her father and Liza dating.

"I like to flatter myself that you're a kind of protégée." Liza gave a little laugh.

Zoe nodded, but there was something in the woman's voice. Zoe glanced up and saw the concern etched in Liza's face.

"What is it? What's wrong?" Zoe asked.

Liza searched the teen's eyes as if trying to make sense of it. "You rolled your sleeves up earlier and I couldn't help noticing the marks on your arm."

Rather than withdraw, Zoe looked back at her, bewildered.

"Wait a minute. You mean, my dad didn't tell you?"

"Tell me what?" Liza responded, puzzled. "I haven't spoken to your father for a couple of days. I think he's a little angry with me," she said, looking away.

"Why? What did *you* do?" Zoe asked with a frown.

Liza held on to the large layout table with photographs strewn haphazardly across its surface.

"When you ran away I knew you were pretty upset with both of us," Liza explained warily. "I told your dad that his relationship with you mattered more than he and I dating." She shrugged.

Zoe was confused. She leaned on the table, knocking one of the photos to the ground. "You mean, you aren't going to see each other anymore and you're doing it because of me?"

"Of course." Liza nodded, putting away some negatives in a folder and placing them in a drawer.

Mulling this news over, Zoe was uncertain about how she felt. On the one hand, she liked having that kind of impact. It meant her feelings mattered. But right on the heels of that reaction came another. She looked at Liza. "Why do you like him?" she asked.

Liza turned back and saw the open curiosity in the teen's eyes.

"Well . . ." She took a deep breath and exhaled. "He's complicated, your dad, even a little bit of a pain in the ass, if you know what I mean?" She grinned.

"Oh, yeah." Zoe laughed, shaking her head. "I know."

Liza switched off a light directed at a wall of pictures and turned back. "But he was like a different person when he was here looking at the photographs. I watched his face. He turned into someone soft and open, more aware than I thought he'd be."

Zoe raised her eyebrows, not sure if she was about to get too much information.

"When he saw the photograph you took of that little girl," Liza offered, a distant look in her eye, "I don't know, Zoe, he just stopped cold. He was overwhelmed." She glanced back at the teen and figured she might be overexplaining. "Let's just say I think he has potential."

Zoe thought about that and looked down for a long moment. "I've been cutting my arm," she said in a burst. "I just . . . I don't know, things hurt and I guess . . ." She swallowed hard. "When I cut I feel in control of my pain. All the other stuff stops mattering. I get to feel like I'm in charge, even for a few minutes. I *need* to—" She broke off.

"You need to express yourself?" Liza suggested gently.

Zoe looked up into the woman's soft, understanding features. "Yeah," she answered slowly, her words registering, making sense to her. "I know that sounds stupid, right?" she mocked herself, rubbing her arm under her sleeve.

"No," Liza said, drawing closer. "No, it's not stupid, Zoe," she said calmly, sitting on a stool next to her. Liza took a breath.

"There was a time in my life when I cut myself off from family and friends. Didn't eat, didn't care about anything . . ."

"No way." Zoe stared back at her as if such a thing could never have been true.

"Yes," Liza assured her. "But thankfully, I realized I was hurting myself and, somehow, I took the chance to find something that mattered to me." She gestured at the walls filled with pictures. "Who knows . . . ," she said, holding up Zoe's latest photo of an energetic young boy skipping stones along the water. "Maybe you're finding another way to express yourself, too?" Liza smiled hopefully.

Zoe gazed at the photograph she'd taken and then looked back at Liza.

"Do you think it's possible . . ." The teen hesitated. "You know, that I maybe got some talent from my grandmother?"

Liza looked into Zoe's searching eyes. She smiled. "Oh, without a doubt."

Zoe nodded, tears at the corners of her eyes. She was silent for a moment. Then, out of nowhere, she said, "He's not angry with you."

"What?" Liza responded, not following.

"My father. I don't think he's upset with you. It's just"—she shook her head, still not quite believing it—"it's weird but kind of cool. I saw it last night in the studio and couldn't believe it." She broke into a grin. "Hey, want to see what he's up to?"

Liza looked back, eyebrows raised with curiosity. "Definitely."

36

Like a couple of convicts on the lam, Zoe and Liza crouched at the window, peering into the art studio. Shadows and pockets of light forced them to squint. The pair pressed their heads up against the glass, listening intently.

"That's right, Mom," Teddy enthused. "We don't need the brush. Your fingers are like a whole hand of brushes. That's it." He focused intently as Kate drew a line with her index finger. She then looped an arc with her middle finger and finished off the figure by sliding the side of her hand underneath the figure, creating the body of a sailboat.

Liza dropped her jaw, amazed and fascinated.

"There you go," Teddy called out triumphantly as Kate's fingers dabbed and swept color across the canvas.

Zoe observed how her grandmother sat back, studying what she had done, cocking her head at different angles. She couldn't be sure, but it appeared as if the woman was hyperventilating. Her shoulders rose and fell in rapid clips.

"Paint what you see. Isn't that what you used to tell me, Mom?" Teddy said as he poked his fingers in the air, copying her movements on an invisible canvas.

It seemed to Liza that Teddy had tapped into some special space, not only in his mother but within himself as well. His arms were gesturing in the air, he was bouncing on his toes; he seemed utterly alive.

As Teddy leaned down toward his mother's ear, both Liza and Zoe pushed closer to the open window to hear what he was saying.

"Paint for me, Kate," he urged. "Paint what you see . . ."

Zoe pulled back, her breath running ragged through her. She had never heard such passion and joy in her father's voice before. She glanced over at Liza, and was struck by the emotion on Liza's face. Turning back, Zoe saw her dad wiping off her grandmother's arm with a towel in order to apply fresh paint. Here, now, in this moment, it seemed her dad had no ulterior motives. There was no one to impress. No media or bimbos or campaign staff, not a prospective voter in sight. Something inside her told her she was watching the real thing. Pressing her head to the window again, she was drawn to the scene in front of her as if to a dream of the person she had always wished he could and would be.

Liza's eyes remained on Teddy, her breathing shallow to better hear, her face hugging the cool surface of the levered outer window. This is what she had glimpsed in Teddy, his sensitivity, his compassion. He had seen the creative impulse still alive in his mother. Some might call it the mark of a good son. But it was more. To Liza it appeared that Teddy had nothing less than the soul of an artist. She turned to Zoe and was startled to find the girl grasping the camera she had begun carrying everywhere.

"Zoe," Liza cautioned.

But for Zoe all else was blocked out. Her eyes were fixed on her father's face as it leaned close to his mother's, his arm outstretched over the older woman's as if guiding her stroke while practicing on an imaginary canvas. Focusing the lens, Zoe quickly took a series of shots.

Liza marveled at the concentration on her student's face, at her instinct to capture the moment unfolding before her. Glancing back into the room, Liza gasped softly. Teddy had turned and was coming right at them.

Panicking, Liza pulled Zoe down to the ground, her heart pounding. Holding their breath, the two waited as Teddy closed the window above them. Crawling on all fours, they quickly made their getaway, giggling like two small children.

37

On the morning of July 3, nearly three weeks after arriving on island, Teddy gazed at the canvas before him. Kate had managed to fill it with crude yet colorful shapes of fish, rudimentary circles suggesting the moon and sun, Rorschach-like handprints that, depending on the pressure and hues she employed, appeared to depict patches of sand or dabs of light. He nodded with satisfaction.

"You're ready," he acknowledged solemnly.

Kate looked up with a tentative smile as she watched her son cross over to a canvas that he had hidden behind a door for the past three days. Lifting it up, he came back and placed his mother's unfinished painting before her. Kate stared at it for a moment as if faced with a daunting task she had no idea how to tackle. She was holding back like she was afraid of it.

Teddy kneeled down by her side and she turned to him. "You're ready, Mom." He nodded. "How about it?"

Kate gazed into his hopeful face and slowly a smile spread over hers. She raised her eyebrows as if to say, *Do you really think I can do this?*

Teddy could read her mind, and he began to nod his head. "You can do this." He grinned.

Kate took a deep breath and turned back to her canvas. As she studied it, her brow wrinkled with strain, as if she were preparing for some private battle. After a moment, her face visibly lightened. She cocked her head to one side, running her fingers over her lips, deliberating. Holding his breath, Teddy watched as she selected the color she wanted and dabbed it on her arm. Dipping her hand into the paint, Kate lifted her index finger to the unfinished spaces in and around the Impressionist-style ocean scene she had previously completed, and, with a deep breath, she began.

Teddy stood back in awe. As far as he was concerned, his mother had just fought off her demon of fear that in touching her unfinished work with paint again she would ruin it. It was as if she needed to let go of what was controlling her—the fear, the unconscious awareness that she had become someone different—in order to return to her art. Watching her come alive as she threw herself into finishing her uncompleted painting, Teddy realized he had somehow found his way back. You could go home again. It was as a boy that he had stood transfixed, thrilling to the sight of his mother creating worlds on canvas. He felt close to her now, as if the thick fog that had separated them had begun to clear. For the first time since his youth, Teddy could see her in her glory.

His heart felt more buoyant, but there were empty spaces that his mother alone couldn't fill. Teddy turned and walked to the window. He gazed out to sea and took a deep breath. It was high time.

There were others he needed to reach out to now. If they would let him.

38

As always, Main Street in Nantucket was closed to traffic on July 4. Making his way through the crowd, Teddy recalled how the island liked to celebrate America's birthday in a big way. He remembered from his youth the dunking contests, smoky barbecues, and fireworks on the beach. He knew that Zoe had never seen anything like it and was happy when she agreed to join him. He watched closely now as she took in the festivities being played out along the closed-off cobblestone center of town.

Children and adults alike were competing in an old-fashioned pie-eating contest, burying their faces into tins of blackberry pies, coming up for air only at the whistle, cheeks and chins and T-shirts covered in rich purple berries. Patriotic music blared from large speakers mounted on the bed of a truck. Red, white, and blue balloons festooned lampposts and the fronts of boutiques and restaurants, occasionally pulling loose and floating up against the brilliant blue sky. Once a year, if you wanted to find Norman Rockwell's America, here it was.

"I'm glad you called," Liza said, greeting Teddy outside Mitchell's Book Corner, near the top of the street.

"You look great," Teddy replied. Then quickly remembering past mistakes, he added, "Don't take that the wrong way."

Liza grinned. "Easy, boy. I took it the right way."

Teddy turned, his eyes fixed on Zoe, who stood twenty feet away in the middle of the closed-off Main Street, focusing her camera on a tiny cherub having her face painted in bright colors by a local volunteer dressed as a clown.

Liza studied him. He seemed like a different man, gentler, more open. And she was touched at the way he kept gazing off at his daughter, as if he were truly enjoying being with Zoe.

"She's very much like her mother," Teddy said quietly as they stood on the curb away from the bustling action.

Liza looked up at him, surprised by his admission. It was the first time he'd mentioned his ex-wife.

"Do you ever miss being married?" she asked, observing his furrowed brow.

"To her mother?" Teddy smiled sadly. "No. We wanted different things from our marriage." He shook his head, recalling the abyss that had grown between them. "Miranda was always planning the next big trip, the next big purchase for the house. And," he paused, exhaling slowly, "she had this neurotic need to have me around all the time."

"And you," Liza prodded gently, "what did you want from the marriage?"

Teddy thought for a moment, his eyes still on Zoe midway across the cobblestone street in front of him. "Out," he said.

Teddy suddenly noticed Frank in a loud Nantucket Red apron, gazing back at him from a bakery booth across the street. He wasn't sure how long the older man had been watching them, but he caught his coy nod of approval before he returned to fishing fresh doughnuts from a small vat of boiling oil.

Teddy turned to Liza. "Care for a cup of coffee?"

The two exchanged knowing smiles, remembering the first time he'd asked her that question. "Sure."

He called out to Zoe to see if she wanted anything. She said she didn't, then waved in his direction, never removing her eye from the camera. He and Liza walked halfway down the block to the Even Keel Cafe and got coffee to go along with a couple of blueberry muffins.

"Are you still working here?" Teddy asked.

"The odd mornings when they need a hand."

Teddy glanced around at the multitudes crowding in the doorway. "This must be one of the busiest mornings they have all summer. Didn't they need you today?"

Liza took a sip from her coffee. "Yeah, they could have used me, but I had a better offer." She grinned. "They understood."

Outside the café they spied Zoe teaming up with another girl from Liza's class. The two were arranging kids for portraits, posing them in front of a rainbow of balloons anchored between old-fashioned lampposts nearby.

"You couldn't get her off the phone or away from her iPod back in L.A.," he said, shaking his head. "I have to hand it to you. Thanks."

"I just taught her a few things," Liza said, sipping her coffee.

"She took what she learned and ran with it." She caught the pensive look on his face. "So how goes the campaign?"

Teddy nearly spilled his coffee. "Hell, I've been so out of it." He shook his head. "My campaign manager is ready to commit hari-kari. The thing is, it meant everything to me. Now, I can't seem to get my head back in the game. Isn't that strange? I should be heading home. I mean, I need to . . ."

Liza gazed at Zoe a dozen feet away. One of the little girls whose picture she'd just taken was giving her a hug. "Maybe you just don't want to?"

"What?"

"Go back to the campaign. Maybe that's not what you were meant to do. If it was your passion you'd know it, don't you think?"

Teddy looked into her eyes. "I wish I could . . ."

Liza held his gaze. "Wish you could what?"

"I don't know." He grinned sadly, looking away. "Spend more time here, give myself a chance to find out who I am now."

A sudden burst of "The Stars and Stripes Forever" began booming from a nearby speaker, sending them fleeing across the street so they could hear each other.

"What's stopping you?" Liza yelled as they ducked into an alcove. He didn't answer, avoiding her eyes. "Teddy, what's stopping you?"

"I have responsibilities I've got to go back to," he insisted as the crowd grew rowdier with the explosion of a noisy cherry bomb. "And then there is the question of you and the possibility of *us*." He looked at her with pained concern. "It seems *us* could only exist here. Would you want to be dating a senatorial candidate? You'd be in the press. Believe me, it's a circus."

Liza looked up at him. "If I really wanted to be with that candidate and it's what he knew in his heart he needed to do, I don't know, maybe. But he'd have to be willing to make me believe it," she said, her eyes searching his. "I can't be with someone who isn't committed. Someone who makes promises he has no intention of honoring."

Teddy couldn't help remembering Judith once saying that he was *exactly* that kind of person. And that only such a person could win the election. The two of them stood in an uncomfortable silence.

At a quarter to twelve, Zoe was surprised to find two fire engines making their way toward each other from opposite ends of Main Street. The excitement in the crowd grew as people chose sides. Some climbed aboard the antique fire engine rolling up the street as others jumped up on a modern version taking its position facing down. Zoe stood between the two trucks separated now by some twenty-five feet. She zeroed her camera in on a child in an overly large fire hat on one truck, snapping the shot, then turned to a mother and daughter on the other who had taken hold of the hose along with dozens of others. Suddenly, powerful jets of water shot from both trucks' hoses, and Zoe realized she was caught smack in the middle of a no-holds-barred Independence Day water fight.

The street exploded with squeals of delight and howls of surprise as volunteer firefighters turned their hoses on the crowd. Zoe did her best to protect her camera with her body but could not seem to escape the attention of one hooting group of teens who had commandeered one of the hoses and was showering her and those around her with a steady blast. Suddenly, Zoe felt herself lifted up by a pair of powerful arms and carried to a safe haven along the curb.

"That was great," she yelled, laughing uncontrollably. Sopping wet, Zoe threw her hair out of her eyes to face her rescuer. She found her father, drenched to the bone, gazing back at her. Her face registered surprise, but, for once, she didn't pull away.

"Thanks," she said softly, biting her lip.

Teddy stood there a bit awkwardly, hesitating to leave while Zoe shifted on the balls of her feet.

"Remember how we used to run through the water sprinklers together?"

Zoe nodded, a smile flitting across her face. "I was like six. You were the only dad who'd get wet with the rest of the kids on the street."

"Yeah." Teddy nodded, looking at her a moment as if she were still that six-year-old.

Zoe noticed Liza across the street, waiting. Teddy followed her gaze and waved.

"It's okay," Zoe said, nodding toward Liza. "Go. But if you ask me, she's got weird taste in men." She gave him a coy shrug and hurried off.

Dripping wet, Teddy stared after her with an appreciative shake of his head. Then he started back, hopping over the hoses now lying spent in the middle of the street.

"You're a lucky guy, even if you're drenched," Liza said. "Some people don't ever get a second chance."

Teddy contemplated her comment and the sadness on her face. He realized he'd been so stuck in his own life that he hadn't the slightest idea what she'd gone through in hers.

"I know I've been caught up in my own drama and I've never really asked about you. What you've gone through. Your past."

Liza remained silent. She began walking and he followed her down the street.

"You can trust me," he said, catching up with her.

"You've got a campaign to get back to, Teddy," she insisted. "You've got a lot on your plate."

"Whoa. Hold on," he said, searching her face as people milled around them. "I want to know more about you," he said, taking her hand. "Don't do this."

Liza turned to him. Teddy could see a vulnerability in her eyes he'd never noticed before. She seemed to be probing him, as if she wanted to believe she could trust him. Slowly, she nodded and gave his hand a squeeze.

"Okay, Teddy." She smiled.

There was some commotion coming toward them. Teddy looked up. He blanched, knowing exactly what was about to happen. He barely had enough time to turn to her and say, "Liza, I am so sorry . . ."

And then, like a bird of prey, a film crew swooped in on them, enveloping Liza and Teddy in its crush.

"Mr. Mathison, Christine Hathaway from station KNBC in Los Angeles," the reporter said, thrusting a microphone into his face. "We've flown here because up until now you've been the leading candidate for your party's nomination. With the primary election less than six weeks away, can you confirm or deny reports that you have dropped out of the race?"

Teddy looked at Liza, stunned. Her face was flushed, her eyes wide as she stared at the media pack pressing in. Teddy held her hand tightly as curious spectators began to crowd closer.

"I . . . ," he began, swallowing hard, looking from the reporter back to Liza.

"Mr. Mathison, can you confirm or deny?"

Teddy opened his mouth but nothing came out.

The reporter shook her head. "It's the Fourth of July. Do you have a message for the voters back in California?"

Teddy's mind was racing as he looked at Liza, who seemed to be waiting for an answer as well. With great effort, he drew a deep breath, composing himself, then turned back to the reporter.

"I want to go on record as saying I have not left the campaign." His voice had taken on the smooth, measured tones of the charismatic candidate. "I am a great believer in the promise of democracy and we're here to celebrate that." He broke into a grin, suddenly playing to the camera.

Liza stared at him as if he were a stranger. The transformation was remarkable. She slowly let go of his hand. Teddy turned to her.

The reporter caught the human drama going on before her and jumped in. "Could you introduce us to your friend,

Mr. Mathison?" She pressed, pushing the microphone at Liza.
"Could you . . . Miss, who are you?"

Liza shook her head. She gave Teddy one last look, then
turned and pushed her way back through the crowd.

"Mr. Mathison?" the reporter insisted, the mike jamming up
into his face. "Teddy, who was that woman? Can you tell the
people back home?"

Teddy looked behind him, but Liza was already gone. Dis-
concerted, he wiped his brow and gazed back into the camera.

"I'm sorry . . . what was the question?"

39

That evening Frank steered the boat through the darkness out into the harbor by Coatue. The sail was down and he had used the motor to take Kate, Zoe, and Teddy out for the annual fireworks spectacular that evening.

"Why isn't Liza joining us?" Frank asked.

"She's tied up with something or other," Teddy said, zipping his Windbreaker.

The older man noticed the pain on Teddy's face and shook his head. "It's always better viewing it out here," he said, changing the subject as Teddy helped him drop anchor.

Up at the front of the boat, nestled in blankets, Kate sat with Zoe beside her, holding on gently. The girl had wanted so badly to include her grandmother and a reluctant Teddy had agreed to go along.

As he pulled up the motor, Frank studied Teddy's somber face. He'd been in some other world the entire trip over from Sconset.

"Your mother's nearly finished her painting, thanks to you, boy," he said. "Why the long face?"

Teddy scratched the back of his head and stared out at the darkening waters.

Frank nodded. "I see. You know, your mother used to brood like you're doing now. Never knew what was going on in that head of hers, only that a person wasn't welcome to know," he said, shaking his head with a smile.

There was a sadness hanging on Teddy as he looked up and saw Zoe chattering softly with Kate. What could they possibly be talking about? Frank followed Teddy's gaze, his eyes focusing on Kate, who appeared fixated on the ripples in the ocean.

"I've always loved her, you know," the Irishman said abruptly.

The words drew Teddy from his thoughts. He turned and looked at the older man. He had long suspected as much, but Frank had never revealed his true feelings. Not in words, anyway.

"I started working at your house, doing odd jobs. I'd catch sight of your mother working back there in the studio." Frank lifted his cap and ran a hand across his head before putting the cap back in place.

"I was amazed a person could do the things she did. Create places and people out of thin air." He cleared his throat as the boat bobbed lightly in the water.

Teddy could see the sadness in the man's face and the faraway look in his eye.

"When your mother was going through everything with your father, we got pretty close," Frank continued, keeping his voice low. "But nothing was ever going to happen. She was too stubborn. After your father's death she just clammed up. All she cared about was you and your sister and her paintings." The Irishman sat up, scratching the side of his face. He gave a sad laugh. "We've been great friends. But I never told her how I felt." He shook his head. "You believe that? Loved the woman for thirty years and never said a thing. Now"—he exhaled—"it's too late."

"Frank . . . ," Teddy said.

The older man shook his head. "I wish I believed in miracles. But I've seen too much." He turned to Teddy, searching his eyes. "I was a damn fool. You hear me?" he said fiercely.

Teddy stared back, surprised at the man's intensity.

"Don't you make the same mistake," Frank warned. "You love a woman, you tell her. You don't let her disappear without knowing what's in your heart."

Darkness had fallen as the first of the fireworks began exploding in the sky over Nantucket. Teddy watched the first flashing light bounce across Frank's face. His ears were ringing with the crackle and roar of the island's celebration. Gazing at the sky, Teddy saw the night light up with purple and gold and silver. He felt the boat rocking beneath him. His mother and Zoe were oohing and aahing, Kate laughing as she pointed at the sky in childish delight. Teddy looked back at his family's oldest friend and saw how Frank's eyes were trained on Kate. He felt as if his heart would explode like the fireworks overhead.

Later that night, Teddy quietly entered his mother's bedroom and then Zoe's, kissing each on the forehead as she slept. He lay awake in his own bed, unable to sleep. He knew there was more work he needed to do with his daughter. Her psychologist had e-mailed articles on self-mutilation for him to read, and he would have to address it, along with other issues.

Judith had phoned to congratulate him on the good film footage that had aired in California. She reminded him to review material for the upcoming debate, warning that he would have to earn back the support of the party pols and a knockout debate performance would be key. Yet right now Teddy wasn't thinking of that. Not the campaign or his mother's nearly completed painting or even the fun he'd had rescuing Zoe from the water fight that morning.

He was thinking of Liza.

40

Shortly after dismissing her class at five, Liza left the Nature Reserve Center. Coming down the steps, she bent over to pick up a leaflet one of the students had dropped. Tucking it into her shoulder bag, she started out again and was surprised to find Teddy slowly emerging from the forest trail facing her. In his hand was a single pink rose. She stared at it.

"Hmm. Nice move," she said.

"Thanks."

"So what do we do now?" Liza asked, studying his face.

"You forgive me and we pick up where we were before the cameras came yesterday?" he offered hopefully.

Liza looked at him. She had stayed awake all night trying to write him off, telling herself he was bad news, that he didn't know what he wanted and she was just going to get drawn into a quagmire.

"It's all right, Teddy. You have someplace to be and it's called California. Let's just . . ."

Teddy took a step forward. "No," he said. "I don't have anyplace I have to be and there's no place I'd rather be. I got cornered yesterday. I should have been able to handle that differently. I'm sorry. I haven't worked out all the details about when I have to leave or what I'm doing. But I'm here now. And I'm just asking for a chance to get to know you better if you wouldn't mind so much."

Liza took a deep breath. She hadn't expected him to show up like this, refusing to go quietly. She exhaled loud enough for him to hear. Then she walked over and stood in front of him.

"Well?" she said.

"Well, what?"

"Are you going to give me the flower?" she replied, waiting.

Teddy smiled. "Here," he said, handing it to her.

Liza brought the pink petals to her nose and inhaled. "Okay." She nodded. "Let's go."

To Teddy's surprise she led him around to the back of the center, where several bicycles were locked up. Placing her rose in the basket of one, she unlocked another and handed it to a bewildered Teddy.

"Where are we going?" he asked.

"You talk too much," she quipped, climbing on her bike and tearing off for the trail.

Teddy watched her, dazed. Then, with a sudden ferocity, he climbed onto his bike and raced to catch up. By the time they had hit the path on Polpis Road, he was already hot on her trail.

Liza led him down around the rotary, above the town, and out onto the road that would take them to the other side of the island. They rode in silence for nearly a half hour, Teddy wondering all the while exactly what was going on. She had already proved she was different. He settled back, happy simply to be in her company.

Liza pulled over at a clearing along the road to Madaket and ditched her bike. Teddy followed suit. Grabbing hold of his hand, Liza dragged him out into the spectacular open fields overlooking Nantucket Sound. They hiked through forest and tall grass, pausing to glimpse the ocean from a lookout station built by the University of Massachusetts. Liza pointed to children luring snapping turtles from a pond with chicken legs dangled from fish line. Teddy could recall Frank teaching him a similar trick as a boy over at Quidnet Pond, closer to Sconset. Pushing onward, Liza pointed to the development of new and expensive homes in the distance.

"People buy up the land and put up homes they use maybe two, three times a year," Liza said, shaking her head, as they sat on a bluff on the South Shore, overlooking the Atlantic. "The island's gotten too expensive for the year-rounders who keep it up. It's not the same place it was when you were a kid, is it?"

"Why do you stay?" he asked.

"It's *my* home. Not theirs," she stated emphatically. "I take these photographs and I have this notion that someone with the money and pull to do something will want to preserve the Nantucket I love, that I can make a difference. Crazy, huh?" She laughed a rich laugh that Teddy loved.

"Wait a minute," Teddy said as it dawned at him. "When I was a kid, Frank used to tell me about the early settlers on this island. The Coffin family, the Husseys, and the Swains. That's you?"

Liza looked over at him, impressed.

"They spelled Swain with a 'y' back then. Richard Swayne came in 1659."

She held his gaze. "Yeah, our family's been here a long time."

He studied her sitting amid a backdrop of evergreen, the magnificent Atlantic spread out below. Liza's spirit seemed timeless, as if the infinite possibility she embodied had always been on the island and always would remain. Yet he again felt that sadness in her. Suddenly, she got up.

"Come on," she said. Together they walked back to the bikes and headed down to Madaket Beach. They stopped en route and Teddy picked up a few sandwiches and a couple of Cisco Amber Whalers.

"Ah, I see you're a connoisseur of true taste." Liza grinned at the sight of the local beer.

They biked on until they'd found a secluded sand dune. Teddy opened the bottles of beer and handed her one.

"To you," he toasted, turning introspective. "For all you've done for Zoe." He held her gaze. "To your passion."

"And to finding yours," Liza affirmed, lifting her bottle to his.

Teddy eyed her as they sipped their beer. "So, ever been married?"

"No." She shook her head. "Never made it that far."

Teddy sensed a deeper story and took a chance. "But you were close?"

Liza ran her fingers down through her hair absentmindedly, her face taking on a faraway look.

"That's all right," Teddy said quickly, fearing he'd made her uncomfortable. "I don't need to know . . ."

"No," she said. "I started to tell you yesterday . . ." She looked out at the surf making its way to shore. "He was a local boy. We'd grown up together, gone to the high school here. Tim always wanted to be a pilot. We used to hang out at the airport, watch the planes land and take off." She laughed self-consciously. "God, how parochial that must sound to a guy who's lived for years in a big city like L.A."

"No, no," Teddy protested. "It's really"—he searched for the words—"kind of romantic." But the bigger pond side of him couldn't help adding, "You know, in an old-fashioned, World War Two sort of way."

She shot him a playful glance. "We'd made a promise to one another to come back here. He'd have his pilot's license and we'd marry, raise kids, the whole dream. When I left the island for Tufts, Tim went to aviation training in North Carolina. After he finished, he flew small planes for a start-up charter group along the East Coast until my graduation in eighty-eight. We both moved back in time for the July wedding. It was going to be here, on the beach at Madaket, at sunset. Corny, I know . . ."

"No, it's not," Teddy insisted, thinking of his mother's affinity for sunsets in this place.

Liza leaned on a knee as she watched a flock of geese flying low over the water in a V formation. "The day before the wedding we were all going crazy. My family's a little nuts and we were toasting, having pillow fights. My girlfriends threw me a 'shower,' literally." She smiled. "Took me right out of bed that morning, carried me to the bathroom, and turned the water on full force."

Teddy noticed how the breeze played with her hair. But his focus was drawn back to the sadness in her eyes.

"My dad told me that other than marrying my mom and having my brother and me, this time was the best of his life." Liza gave a half-smile and grew quiet.

He watched the emotions playing across her face. It seemed to Teddy that she was going someplace she didn't want to visit but had decided to because he'd asked.

"Tim had a charter from the island up to Bangor, Maine, that afternoon. It was a new four-seater the company had just bought and he was pretty thrilled about taking it out. With the wedding the next day, he'd insisted on hopping over to New Hampshire to pick up his grandparents. It was evening when they left Manchester for Nantucket." She paused, gathering the strength for the next part. "A fog had started forming around sunset. We'd spoken before they took off, but Tim had no worries. An hour later I was leaving our family clambake to pick them up and that's when the call came. The plane had disappeared off the coast of Nantucket. They didn't know if Tim got disoriented in the fog or if the new instruments weren't functioning . . ." Liza took a breath and let it out softly. "It was ten days before they found the wreckage and we got to bury them." She looked away. "When the Kennedy tragedy happened off Martha's Vineyard I relived it all. No one should know that heartache."

Teddy sat there stunned, trying to fathom her pain. He didn't look away from her as they sat in silence. He wondered how someone could go through that kind of a tragedy and come out the other end. He was in awe that she had managed to embrace a life of creativity after such a blow, to keep her passion alive. The thought called to mind another woman, an artist he knew well, who had lost the man she loved long ago.

"How did you deal with all of it?" he asked quietly. They both noticed the tenderness in his voice.

Liza glanced over at him with a strong, determined grin. "You cry a lot. There are unbearable pools of sadness. You get angry. You shut down. I didn't want anything to do with anyone. Practically starved myself for a while. Eventually, you find you don't much like yourself like that," she explained, taking a deep breath. "When you get there you have a choice." She paused. "Let it take you down, or allow the hurt to become a part of you." She nodded, remembering it.

"Seems to me you'd always be in pain that way," Teddy said as his eyes searched hers.

"No," she said, shaking her head firmly. "No, the pain turns into memory. And you honor that memory by living, I think." She nodded, tears forming in her eyes. "By creating, because that's you. It's who you are."

Teddy recalled the words his mother had shared with him. "You have to become what you were born to be . . ."

Liza turned to him, surprised. "Yes," she said, her eyes soft and earnest. "My photographs are like my blood. They pump life into me. I see kids like Zoe, young artists who have the gift, and it feeds something in my soul. Does that make sense?"

Teddy reached out and took her hand. He was touched deeply by all she had endured. They sat in silence for several minutes. Feeling her hand in his set off a reaction within him. A deep ache took hold. He, too, was losing someone.

"My mother's disappearing right in front of me," he said. "And I can't make it stop . . ."

Liza reached out, drawing him closer, enveloping him in her arms, feeling the emotion surging through him. "Ssh. Ssh. You're more powerful than you know, Teddy," she whispered. "Look at what you've done. Your mother's painting again," she said, holding him tightly. "And Zoe, Zoe's amazing. You've given her that chance. You are doing remarkable things," Liza said with conviction. "You're helping create light where there wasn't any. That's the mark of an artist . . ."

She held him in her arms as their embrace became something else. His hand gently caressed her back, her neck, her head. Teddy found himself asking, "Have you ever been in love again?"

"I talk a good game," Liza said. "But no. Deep down I'm a coward. I haven't really been willing to trust it, you know?"

Teddy pressed her close to him. "Yes," he said softly. "I know."

And, like that, it happened. It was simple, natural, unplanned. Teddy turned to her and their lips met in one long, all-encompassing kiss.

Liza suddenly pushed him down and rose to her feet. Bursting into laughter, she bolted across the sand, removing her

T-shirt and shorts as she went, and ran into the ocean. As she dove into a wave, Teddy stood silently in awe. Throwing caution to the wind, he dashed for the water, too, tearing off his shirt and slacks and galloping into the surf. Splashing playfully, they reached for each other as the waves broke against their bodies. Teddy pressed his face next to Liza's and took in the glorious sunset, the light playing across the ocean's surface.

"It's the light that makes them dance," he whispered.

"What?" Liza laughed at the odd comment.

Teddy grinned, pulling her closer. And with their feet barely touching the ocean bottom, he danced her in a circle as the water lapped their limbs and their lips found each other once again.

41

The sixth of July. Two days to the debate. One month and a week to the special primary back in California. Teddy did the requisite three early-morning interviews with radio stations in Sacramento, L.A., and San Diego, but his mind was on the event later in the day. There was to be a small gathering, a viewing in the late afternoon of Kate Longley Mathison's newest work of art. He had invited Liza and Frank, as well as his mother's physician, Dr. Jennings, to join Annie, Zoe, and, of course, the artist herself.

As Teddy and Annie helped Kate to the seat of honor on the back lawn, she appeared tired and a little dazed. Teddy hoped that today of all days she could take some satisfaction in her accomplishment.

There was a light breeze as a seagull took up residence on the white gate at the path leading down to the ocean. Annie brought out a tray of champagne and placed it on a small, round wooden table nearby as Zoe served cheese and crackers to her grandmother and the others.

Liza approached the older woman.

Teddy noticed and walked over. "Mom?" he said. She didn't look up. "Kate?" he tried again. Slowly, his mother lifted her head. "I'd like you to meet another artist. She's a woman who reminds me a great deal of you."

Liza knelt down in front of her and gently took the older woman's hand. "It's an honor to meet you, Kate," she said. "I've been a fan of your work for a very long time."

Teddy smiled at the sight of these two formidable women meeting. He felt a pang, wishing the circumstances were different, that these women he cared about could truly know each other. He watched as his mother eyed Liza blankly, smiled, and then looked away.

Liza got to her feet and gave him a small hug. Teddy nodded. He had placed a white sheet over the painting and easel on the grass in the middle of the lawn, hoping Kate would unveil her work. But when the time came, he realized it was going to be up to someone else to do the honors.

"Zoe," Teddy suggested. "I think your grandmother would like it if you unveiled her painting."

The request surprised her. Turning to Kate, Zoe made her way over to her and knelt down beside the large Adirondack chair.

Kate looked into her granddaughter's eyes. "Hello," she remarked pleasantly, as if to a stranger.

"We're here to see your painting, Grandma," Zoe said with a little smile.

"Really?" Kate laughed. Was she following any of this?

"Dad's asked me to unveil your work," she explained in a slow, clear voice. "Is that all right with you?"

Kate reached out to touch Zoe's eager young face.

"Hello, sweet girl. Now whose girl are you again?" she said, completely lost.

Zoe gazed back into the older woman's face, a flicker of pain in her eyes.

"It's all right, Zoe," Teddy said gently.

The others gathered in a semicircle, shifting uncomfortably at the sight of the artist unable to recognize her own grand-daughter. But Zoe refused to budge, stubbornly waiting for her grandmother's signal.

"I'm *your* girl, Grandma," she said firmly. "I'm your grand-daughter, Zoe."

Kate studied her. "My granddaughter?" she questioned. A hint of recognition flitted across her face as if, for a second, the identity had registered. But then it quickly vanished.

"I'm going to unveil your painting; is that all right with you?" Zoe persisted. She searched her grandmother's eyes as if she might *will* her to stay focused.

"Zoe," Teddy softly prodded. "It's okay. She doesn't need to . . ."

"*I* need her to say it," Zoe insisted. "It's the only time I'll . . ." Her voice caught in her throat. "I need her to say it, okay? To know I'm here."

"It's a struggle for her, Zoe," Annie said quietly as she stood nearby. "But she knows you're here, I'm sure of it."

Liza wanted to go to her, to comfort Zoe, but thought it probably wasn't her place. She looked at Annie, who stood motionless a few feet away, and then at Frank, whose eyes remained on the covered easel as if he couldn't quite believe there was a completed painting beneath it.

Zoe looked up into her grandmother's face. The old woman remained beyond her reach. Zoe got up slowly and walked over to the easel. Taking hold of the corner of the sheet, she stared at her grandmother with a pained expression and then gently pulled it off of the canvas.

"My God," Frank uttered.

Dr. Jennings, Annie, Liza, and Zoe drew closer. They were looking at a canvas that had clearly been painted by two different artists. There was an Impressionistic layer that was the original ocean scene, specks of light reflecting off the water that could be conjured only by a master. Rich uses of purple, gold, yellow, and magenta, indicating a sunset of spectacular dimension. There was a line of seagulls gracing the sky and a romantic couple arching toward each other in a boat. They were all created with brushstrokes that were detailed and refined, along with delicate flourishes that added texture and depth to the depiction of the body of water, lending it the "feel" of movement.

The accomplished portion of work filled the upper two-thirds of the canvas save for a swatch in the upper right corner. Against the upper scene was a newer, primitive overlay of bold colors, reds and yellows and blues that took the shape of fish, two sailboats, a whale. In the top right corner was a crude but striking round ball of light, half-gold, half-white, as if sun and moon were sharing the same space for a moment as they exchanged places. The bottom third of the canvas depicted a rough texture of sand made up of varying shades of brown, white, and black that had been formed by a series of handprints, one atop the other, spreading toward the water. On the sand, there was a crude outline of what looked like a young girl, her frame drawn in black. Inside this figure, and filling her in, were a series of bright squiggles; almost tribal, composed of orange and white. It was utterly unique. Even more, it was beautiful.

"My word," Annie sighed, shaking her head.

"I had no idea such a thing was possible given the circumstances," Dr. Jennings marveled, looking over at Teddy, then back at Kate in astonishment.

"Grandma," Zoe responded, awestruck.

Liza moved next to Teddy, squeezing his hand and whispering, "It's unbelievable."

"It's a masterpiece, Kate," Frank said. "Bravo," he called out, breaking into applause.

"Who is this?" Annie said, pointing to the figure of the young girl.

Teddy looked at his daughter, whose eyes were fixed on the figure.

"Zoe," came the frail voice from behind them.

Everyone turned back toward the artist as she sat alert now, leaning forward, gesturing to the canvas. "That's my granddaughter . . . Teddy's girl," she suddenly stated as if it were perfectly obvious.

Zoe stared at the canvas in amazement, then looked up into her father's eyes. A wave of emotions threatened to burst through her skin. She wanted to go to him, to thank him for bringing her to the island so she could know her grandmother, for believing it was possible the woman could paint again, for not giving up and treating Kate as if she were already dead.

Annie came over and gazed gratefully up into Teddy's eyes. "You know someone through their actions," she reminded him with a smile. "Thank you, *Teddy.*"

Suddenly, Kate, who had been nibbling on a cracker with cheese, began coughing, loud and raspy, doubling over in a jerky contraction. All eyes turned to her. Dr. Jennings patted her back, calling for water.

"What are you doing?" she stammered at the doctor as she fought to draw breath. "Stop that," she coughed and then broke into hoarse spasms as Annie handed the doctor a glass of water.

"There you go, Kate," Dr. Jennings said calmly, placing the water to her lips. "Easy does it." He reached for his medical bag nearby.

"Mom," Teddy called out, moving to her. "What's happened?" he demanded of Dr. Jennings.

"In the later stages of Alzheimer's some patients may forget how to swallow," the doctor explained quietly. "You have to be careful what you give her and make sure she remembers to chew her food."

Zoe looked on, visibly upset. "I served that to her," she said, frightened.

"You couldn't have known. I wasn't even sure how far this illness had progressed." Dr. Jennings listened to the old woman's chest with his stethoscope and frowned. "Her lungs have some fluid in them. My guess is she's contracted an infection. I'll do a test and send it to the lab, but I'm pretty sure," he said as Kate calmed down, closing her eyes. "Respiratory problems like pneumonia often occur with the progression of this illness."

"Shouldn't we get her to the hospital?" Liza asked with deep concern.

Dr. Jennings shook his head. "No, I don't think so."

"What do you mean?" Zoe called out. "We took her to the hospital when she fell . . ."

"I know, Zoe," Dr. Jennings said softly, crossing to her. "That was different. We may have had to set some bones or deal with a concussion in that case, but Kate and I spoke of this a long time ago. She didn't wish to leave her home nor have extraordinary measures used to fight these infections, if and when they came."

"When did she say this?" Teddy wanted to know. "Frank?" he looked at the older man.

Frank nodded. "Joanna told me about it. Kate signed a paper to that effect a while back. Annie knows."

Teddy looked to the caretaker, who solemnly nodded her head. He felt Liza's hand on his shoulder.

"Well, we can change that, can't we?" Teddy insisted. "Frank, you're the executor of her will. Someone must have power of attorney to make medical decisions, don't they?" he demanded, looking from the doctor to Frank and Annie.

"She named two," the Irishman answered. "Joanna's one," Frank said as he walked over to Teddy. "You're the other."

"Me?" Teddy said in disbelief. "But why didn't anybody . . . ?"

"Joanna fought your mother on it but Kate insisted. Your sister thought you'd make a commotion. Never figured you'd want or have to know. I have the papers, but it doesn't matter, because you're not going to do anything," Frank said.

"You heard the doctor. This infection could kill her. I can demand that they treat her."

"It's not what she wants," Frank insisted, his stoic face barely hiding the weight of his emotions. "You understand that, don't you? It's not what *she* wants."

"She may improve a little," Dr. Jennings explained quietly to those assembled. "But I'm afraid, given her wishes, that her condition will soon worsen." He turned to Teddy. "You have to know—it's truly astounding what you've accomplished with her."

With a swiftness that surprised everyone, Zoe let out a small cry and rushed to her father, wrapping her arms around him as she buried her face in his chest. Teddy stood there utterly amazed. Faltering, having had little practice, he gently placed a hand on her head to soothe her. He gazed into Frank's eyes. The older man nodded back, like a proud father. Teddy looked over at Liza. She stood a few feet away, visibly moved, knowing how much this must mean to him for his daughter to seek comfort in his arms, how difficult the news about his mother had to be.

"There we go now," the doctor said as Kate looked blankly at those around her.

"What's this?" she asked weakly, as if awaking from a nap. "What are we supposed to be doing now?"

Teddy led Zoe over to her. Encouraging everyone to take some champagne, he solemnly lifted his glass in a toast. "To my mother, the great artist," he said with pride as emotion coursed through him. "Here's to Kate," he said, the words nearly catching in his throat. "The Queen of Nantucket."

"To Kate," the others responded.

His heart was beating loudly within him as Teddy sipped the bubbly, arm around his daughter, glancing over at Liza a few feet away as she smiled back at him. Looking down at his mother, Teddy hoped she wasn't oblivious to this toast in her honor. Her eyes were on the painting she had completed. The smallest of smiles appeared now on her lips. Teddy felt a tightness in his chest as the reality of losing her and the reality of all those lost years flooded his brain.

42

Awaking with a start, Teddy glanced around, unaware he'd fallen asleep in the rocking chair by his mother's bed. He looked behind him and saw the first rays of dawn. Wiping the sleep from his eyes, he turned back and found the bed was empty.

"Mom?" he called, panic creeping into his voice. Getting up, he checked the bathroom. It was empty. "Kate?" He looked into Zoe's room and found her still asleep. The thought of waking his daughter crossed his mind, but he decided not to. She'd only get upset. No, Kate couldn't have gone far, he assured himself.

He ran up to the roof, afraid she'd wandered up there; but it was empty. Returning to the second floor, he checked his room and then bounded downstairs. Searching the rest of the house, he found no sign of his mother. Pausing by the back porch, Teddy was unnerved. He remembered Frank warning him that Kate had tried on a number of occasions to make it down to the ocean on her own. Teddy rushed out the door onto the back lawn. The gate leading to the beach was ajar. He could only imagine what might happen to her in her weakened state if she'd attempted to make it down the steep incline. As he headed for the bluff, the image of her sprawled out there, alone and frightened or worse, flashed like a horrible nightmare in his brain.

Teddy raced down the trail to the water, cutting his legs on small shrubs. Kate was nowhere in sight. Calling her name repeatedly, he stumbled forward in a panic, limbs akimbo, his eyes darting across the beach below. He spilled out onto the sand and tumbled to the ground. Righting himself, Teddy bolted for the water's edge. He searched the shoreline wildly. Then, pivoting to his left, he saw her. A little figure, dressed in her nightgown, sitting on an upturned, faded red boat on the sand, staring longingly out to sea.

Teddy stopped and stared at her, catching his breath. She looked so serene, so natural, perched on the edge of the boat. He hated to disturb her peace, so he quietly walked over to her.

"You scared me, Mom," he said, his heart beginning to calm. He looked back at the trail he'd stumbled down. "You could have broken your neck. I don't even know how you got down here in your condition. Kate? Can you hear me?"

Kate's eyes remained focused on the morning tide as it ebbed and flowed before her.

"Mom," he called again. Getting no response, he gulped some air and hung his head.

"Swim . . . ," she said softly.

Teddy looked up at her, incredulous. "Are you *kidding* me?"

She turned to him. "Finished . . ."

"What?"

"My painting," she said slowly, working to get the thought out of her. "It's . . ."—she hesitated, squinting to concentrate— ". . . done."

Teddy's breath caught in his throat. He was thunderstruck. Of course, he assured himself. Her ritual. The image of her racing down to the water to celebrate the completion of a new work washed through him. The way she would jump in her boat, row like crazy in a burst of energy, then, hooting and hollering like a young girl, dive into the water. He recalled the sheer, uninhibited joy of her release.

Teddy studied the concentration in her face. Somewhere inside was the recognition that she had, at long last, finished her painting. It was time for her swim. She hadn't forgotten, he marveled. Glancing down now at the upturned, worn red vessel Kate had been sitting on, it all came together. Of course. *Red, red, the boat on its side.* He realized it wasn't nonsense or a fragment of some distant lullaby. Some part of her still clung to her identity.

As he studied the boat he had a sudden urge to take her out on the water. But she's sick, he thought. The doctor had determined there was indeed an infection in her lungs. He could make it worse bringing her out there. Still, watching the longing in her eyes, Teddy felt the same determination to help her that he had experienced in the art studio when she had sat staring at her uncompleted painting. "Want to go for a ride, Mom?" he blurted out.

Helping Kate to her feet, Teddy put his shoulder to the boat and managed to flip it over. The oars tucked under the seats spilled out into the sand.

Kate let out a cry of delight. "Yes," she called to him, bringing her hands together excitedly as if in fulfillment of a prayer. "Red, red, the boat . . ."

With a mighty effort Teddy dragged the boat to the edge of the water, attaching the oars. Lifting his mother in his arms, he gently helped her into the small vessel as she gave a gasp. Pulling off his sweatshirt, he tied it around her shoulders for warmth. Shaking his head as he eyed the whitecaps kicking up out in the ocean, he drew a deep breath and blew it out forcefully.

"Hold on, Kate," he shouted. "Here we go . . ." And with that, Teddy pushed the boat out into the ocean as Kate held on to the side as best she could. Splashing as his heels knifed through the water, Teddy let out a holler and climbed into the boat, nearly falling over as he found his seat opposite his mother. Grabbing hold of the oars, Teddy stared into Kate's face. It was filled with pleasure. He nodded and began to row.

Teddy dug his oars into the water and pulled back hard on them. The morning wind was causing small waves to slam up against the sides of the boat. With great effort, Teddy got them some hundred feet out to sea and paused. Lifted up and down by the undulating motion beneath them, he gazed at his mother, reaching out to steady her. Kate stared down into the water. Teddy saw the perplexed look on her face. It seemed as if she were trying to determine what would happen next.

A moment later she looked up into her son's eyes. "Swim?" she asked softly.

"No," Teddy replied firmly. He realized now that she knew what came next—first the rowboat, then the swim. The boat was rising and falling, and Teddy was angry with himself for having pushed things by trying such a crazy stunt in this weather.

As he reached for the oars to get them back to shore, Kate suddenly rose in her seat and turned toward the water. She appeared ready to jump. Horrified, Teddy dropped the oars and reached out for his mother, scrambling to pull her back down. Fearfully, he held on to her.

"No, Mom," he castigated her as he sat back opposite her, refusing to relinquish hold of her hands. "You can't. I know you want to but you can't. It's not safe for a swim and you're in no condition to take one. You could drown."

The older woman screwed her face up tightly as if she couldn't find the right words. She pulled her hands from his and began tapping her head in frustration. "Listen to me," she said with a sudden urgency. She struck at her head again as if it were her enemy, clenching her teeth together as if to punish her lips for not being able to get out all that she had inside of her. "No more." She squeezed the words out of her like the last remnants from a used-up tube of paint. "Teddy," she begged. "No . . . more!"

Teddy's heart sank within him at the pitiful sight of her suffering. He reached out and took her fists away, lowering them to her side and gently holding them there.

With the sea lifting them and putting them back down, Kate stared into his face, her demeanor growing agitated. "Don't stop me," she called out with a sudden stubbornness, trying to pull her hands from his. "Swim . . . ," she insisted, her eyes pleading with his. "One . . . last . . . swim . . . ," she demanded. "Let . . . go."

No, he responded silently, his lips parting, afraid as he clung to her while the boat bobbed about on the water. He recalled now Frank telling him how his mother had expressed the desire to go for one last swim to end her disease, to simply become one with the ocean she loved. She was still bent on doing it. Gripped with fear, Teddy grabbed hold of the oars and wrestled back control of the boat from the sea. Pulling mightily, he rowed for shore. *No,* his mind rebelled. *Not now. Not when I've finally reclaimed you.*

"I need you to help me," Teddy shouted at her as he rowed, their eyes locked on one another. "I need you, Mom, do you hear me?"

But the older woman's eyes flashed with life. With a scream of determination she willed herself forward, grabbing hold of one of the oars. Kate looked up at her son's stunned face with a clarity that frightened him. "Listen . . . to . . . me," she ordered as the sea sprayed up, drenching both of them. "I . . . don't want to live like this. . . . Help me, Teddy," she pleaded. "Let me . . . go."

Teddy's eyes were wide with alarm. He could see she was using every ounce of her will to remain lucid. Emotion welled up within him. He couldn't allow it. "No!" he screamed. And taking hold of the oars, he rowed with all his strength. In minutes he was jumping from the boat and pulling it ashore. Lifting his mother from the boat, he dragged it free of the water and pushed it back over in the sand.

Teddy turned to his mother. The fight in her had drained away now. She appeared frail and lost. Holding on to her firmly, he guided her up the pathway to the house. His mind raced with the reality of what she was asking. She wanted to die. And she was asking him to help her. But the woman couldn't be thinking right. Hell, she could barely think at all, could she?

As they struggled up the path away from the rough waters, Teddy felt as if *he* were drowning. He was desperate for solid footing. Just as he thought he'd found it, his mother's request was ripping it away.

And yet, as he gazed down at her, it struck him that even in her unsettled state, his mother was somehow clinging to an anchor of certainty—her indestructible sense of identity. He felt a sudden admiration for her. While there might not be a lot about *himself* he was sure of at that moment, one thing seemed absolutely clear—Alzheimer's and all, Kate Mathison knew who she was.

43

Liza had arranged a showing of her students' photographs and each of them was to be introduced. Climbing the steep steps to the second-floor art gallery, Teddy's head swam. His mother's disturbing request in the boat had shaken him to his core. He realized that she had made her intentions clear to Frank back when she was still of sound mind. This was what *she* had wanted. His wanting her to stay alive was selfish, it was for *him*. The knowledge that Kate had given him, along with his sister, power of attorney meant that he could insist on getting her medical attention that might preserve her life. Yet, as the Irishman had pointed out, to do so would be in defiance of his mother's wishes. Teddy chafed at the warning, at being told he was powerless to change things. Still, the questions haunted him. Wasn't it right to rescue her when she could no longer think or act for herself? But was it right to force someone to live beyond her wishes, replacing her will with his own?

As Teddy reached the top of the stairs, his thoughts were interrupted by the overflow crowd milling through the brightly lit space and buzzing about the exhibition.

Zoe had been nervous all day. The truth was, she'd been shy and reticent about being in front of an audience ever since she'd played a mouse in a two-minute skit in preschool and forgot to squeak on cue. She had actually taken off her ears and begun crying, announcing to all assembled that they needed to start the skit over. The resulting laughter from the audience had scared her right off the stage.

Earlier in the day, Teddy had approached his daughter, hoping to encourage her by noting that she herself wouldn't be on display, simply her photographs.

"Same thing," she'd replied.

In truth, she had appeared sad all day, refusing to leave her grandmother's side as the two sat in the art studio. She'd been forced to go only when Liza came by to ask her to lend a hand in setting things up at the gallery. After Zoe left, Kate had looked around as if expecting the girl to return but soon gave up.

Thinking of his mother, Teddy took a deep breath. He was going to be here for his daughter, he told himself, and that meant banishing thoughts of Kate so that he could focus on Zoe.

"Hey, aren't you Zoe Mathison's father?" Liza quipped as she approached him, two glasses of chardonnay in her hand. She handed him one, gazing at the worry on his face. "Cheer up." She smiled. "She's going to be all right."

Teddy knew she meant Zoe and tried to smile.

"Actually, it's my mom I'm worried about." He rubbed his forehead.

Liza placed her hand on his and held his gaze, letting him know she understood.

The touch of her hand felt good, solid, anchoring. Teddy exhaled deeply.

Liza rubbed his hand briskly. There was a gleam in her eye. "I think I've got something you ought to see." She brightened and led him through the crowd.

"Something else?"

Teddy took in the genial gathering: family members of the students along with a smattering of tourists, all examining photographs mounted on large white boards hung against the rustic brick walls of the gallery. Teddy caught glimpses of familiar buildings from around Nantucket on which some of the students had chosen to train their cameras. He recognized the Brant Point Lighthouse and the gleaming spire of the First Congregational Church as well as an aerial view from its tower. There was a large shot of the African Meeting House at Five Corners and another of the Atheneum, Nantucket's library, where Frederick Douglass had given his first public speech.

As Liza tugged him by the hand, Teddy saw a teenager pointing to her work, which consisted of nautical shots—Old South Wharf, sailboats bobbing lazily at anchor in the bay, the bold red and blue chute of a parasailor against a brilliant sky. It reminded Teddy of the date he'd gone on with her, the spectacular, frightening ride they'd taken in tandem.

And then Liza stopped. He followed her gaze and discovered Zoe standing near her own photographs. She appeared to have the largest group of admirers. He gazed at the astonishing scene of people crowding in, marveling at his daughter's work.

Teddy had only seen that first remarkable photograph Liza had shown him, the one of the young girl, vulnerable and brave, staring into the lens. It was haunting and had stopped him cold. He had the same reaction now, seeing it again. But mounted next to it on a different board was one of a young boy skipping stones on the water. There was another of a mother and daughter splashing wildly in the ocean, the drops of water hanging in midair, sparkling like diamonds, showering the picture with light.

"Who's this?" someone asked, pointing to a large rectangular shot composed of shadows with a single, dominating shaft of shimmering sunlight.

Caught in the shadows and light were two figures. The one seated was a woman, her long flowing white hair pouring down her back, her hand poised before a partially completed canvas. The man to her side was standing, leaning over her, his arm arched as if he, too, were painting, only with an invisible brush. Teddy gazed at it, stunned. Zoe had captured this dazzling shot of his mother and himself and made it appear as if they were suspended in time. The blast of light that bathed their figures, angled only partially toward the camera, accentuated the creative act, focusing the eye on the moment of inspiration, poised to paint, rendering everything else to the shadows.

"That's my father and grandmother," Zoe answered, having to clear her throat to speak louder.

"It's about art, then?" an intense, middle-aged woman asked her pointedly.

Zoe shrugged. "I just liked the shot," she said. Then, unable to help herself, Zoe burst into a beaming grin.

Teddy thought his heart would burst right through his chest. He turned to Liza. "Thank you," he said, hugging her tightly as he grew wistful. "I'd do anything if she could be like this from now on," he whispered. "Happy."

Liza drew back, studying him. "You don't control her future, Teddy." She smiled softly. "You can't. You know that. But hey"—she nodded warmly—"something tells me your love is going to make a big difference to her."

Teddy turned to look at Zoe as she shook the hands of some of her admirers. "I'd like to freeze this moment, this one right here," he said.

"That's what photographs do." Liza nodded. "They hold on to the moment. So that when we have to let go"—she drew close—"and the day will come when you have to let her go"—she hugged him—"we can look at our memories . . ."

The thought startled Teddy, causing him to take a deep breath and plunge forward. Zoe stared up at him.

"I'm so proud of you," Teddy said, his eyes filled with emotion.

Zoe broke into a grin. "Thanks. I wish Mom could see this, too."

"She will." Teddy nodded. "This is just the beginning for you." He smiled and, spreading his arms, he quickly pulled her to him.

"The day will come when you have to let her go." Teddy looked back at Liza and their eyes met. Her words pained him, but in his heart he knew they were true. He couldn't help wondering—how do you let a daughter go? Or a mother?

44

All the way back to Sconset, Zoe bubbled with excitement as she relived the thrill she'd just experienced. She called her mother on her cell phone, bubbling over with details of her first exhibition. Teddy could only imagine that Miranda must be very happy to hear the change in their daughter.

He glanced over at Liza in the passenger seat. There was to be a little celebration back at the house in Zoe's honor, and he was glad Liza was joining them. She had brought along Zoe's photographs to share with Kate and Frank, who had stayed behind. Teddy was learning that crowds had a tendency to confuse and agitate those who suffered from Alzheimer's. The brain was simply bombarded with too many stimuli.

As they approached Sconset, Teddy glanced out at the lighthouse, signaling its beacon as if calling him home. He had a sinking feeling in the pit of his stomach. He was about to face Kate again. Would she remember what she'd tried to do that morning? Did she really want him to let her go? Glancing to the side, he saw Liza gazing at him. She seemed aware of the pain he was feeling. There was an urge within him to share it with her. Might she understand his mother's desire to take what was left of her life into her own hands?

He heard Zoe say, "Sure, he's here." She handed her father the phone. Teddy spoke to Miranda and told her of Zoe's remarkable talent and the success that she'd had at the show. He gave her a firm yes when she insisted he support her in getting their daughter back into therapy to deal with Zoe's cutting herself. She expressed the hope they would be back in L.A. as soon as possible and said she was certain his mother's condition was difficult for both him and Zoe. Teddy promised to phone her tomorrow with an update on their return.

"So, you *are* leaving," Liza said when Teddy ended the call.

He could see the emotion in her face. He had never imagined he would remain on island, and now he got jittery at the thought of saying good-bye. But Miranda wanted Zoe back home. And the big debate with the other two candidates was scheduled for tomorrow night. He had all but suspended preparation for it. With Liza's eyes on him and with his deepening connection to his mother, Teddy was desperately torn.

When they pulled into the driveway, Zoe scooped up her photographs and rushed in the door, with Teddy and Liza close behind. But as they entered the studio, Teddy stopped cold. There, sitting across from his mother and Frank, was a striking brunette in a dazzling summer dress offset by a braided gold necklace.

"Hello, Teddy," Judith said.

"What . . . ?" Teddy exclaimed in surprise. "What are you . . . ?"

"I was just explaining to your mother and Frank here that if Mohammed won't come to the campaign trail . . ." She smiled, overly effusive.

Liza caught the bitter undertone in the woman's voice and stiffened.

Judith extended her hand to Liza. "Hi. I'm Judith Mackey, Teddy's campaign manager, and you must be the reason he's still here," she said pointedly. "You see, he's running for the Senate. Well, maybe it would be more accurate to say, running *from* the Senate. And"—she glanced around the room—"here's the real kicker. The campaign's actually *not* in Massachusetts, believe it or not, but in California."

Teddy eyed her, not amused. "Judith, this is Liza Swain. She's a friend."

"*Friend?* Euphemisms really aren't necessary, are they, Teddy?" she asked with a touch of derision.

"What are you doing here?" Teddy asked, reacting to the incongruity of finding his campaign manager in his mother's art studio.

"What am I . . . ? No, no, Teddy." Judith's eyes flashed. "The question is, what are *you* doing here?"

"Look, Judith, I don't know what you think you're up to—" Teddy started, his face turning red, his voice growing combative.

"I know," Judith cut him off coolly. "That's why I'm here. We're going to take that photograph of you and your mother that you came here for," she explained, as if speaking to a child, "and then we are going to head back to California and do our best to salvage what's left of your campaign."

"How dare you!" Teddy demanded, growing enraged.

"Teddy," Liza cautioned, looking at Kate's obviously bewildered but troubled face.

Judith crossed to him. "The game of politics is played best with a cool head and an eye on the prize," she stated under her breath for Teddy's ears only. "I won't let you blow this. We've worked too hard. You need to remember who you are, where your allegiances lie. Now, I don't know what you think you've been doing here while we've been putting out fires back home, but it stops today."

Teddy, his face flushed, his jaw muscles pulsing, eyed her with contempt. He was in no state of mind to be pushed, not by Judith, not by anyone.

"Now, how about that photograph?" Judith announced, producing a camera from her handbag.

"That's a great idea," Frank interrupted, stepping gingerly in between them. "There *should* be a family photograph. That's only right, Teddy," he said, nodding. Turning to him, the older man added softly, "We don't need any trouble in front of your mother, do we, lad?"

"That's my Teddy," came a frail voice behind them.

Everyone looked back at Kate, who was holding a photograph Zoe had handed her of a boy skipping stones.

Liza caught her breath, glancing first at Zoe, then over at Teddy.

"He loves skipping stones." She smiled with satisfaction, turning to Zoe. "Did you see him?"

Zoe didn't know how to answer. Judith cooled her heels and Liza eyed the other woman warily.

"Yes," Frank finally jumped in. "Yes, Kate, she saw him. And guess what? He's right here, your son. And he wants to take a picture with you."

"Really?" Kate answered. "Is he really here?" she asked like a lost little girl.

Teddy gazed down at his mother, his heart full of sadness. He turned back to Judith, who was waiting for him. His eyes next caught Frank's. The older man was giving him that look that said it would be all right and to get on with it. Zoe was next to his mother, her eyes wide with concern, watching his reaction intently. Turning to face Liza, he saw the warmth of her gaze, as if she were holding him even from that distance. Yes, Frank was right, there shouldn't be a scene in front of his mother. Slowly, he moved to take his place next to Kate.

"I'm right here, Mom," he said, kneeling beside her as Zoe and Frank backed away to give them room.

The older woman broke into a smile. "Hi there," she said softly.

Turning back, Teddy watched as Judith lifted her camera to take the shot. But something in him insisted this was wrong. "No," he blurted out.

Judith lowered the camera impatiently.

"I'd like Zoe to take it," he said, turning toward his daughter. "Could you do that for us?"

Zoe was taken off guard but slowly smiled and nodded.

Teddy gazed up at Liza, who was observing from the corner. Off to the side stood the Irishman, his hands clasped together as if he'd been waiting for just such a moment. Teddy glanced over at Judith's expectant face. Yes, she was finally getting the photo she had wanted from the beginning—her candidate as the dutiful son. It would probably be fed to all the media outlets: *Teddy Mathison and his dying mother.* He'd no doubt have a lock on the family values market now, he told himself.

There was a burning sensation in his head. Teddy turned to his mother, suddenly protective, not wanting her to be used. She deserved dignity and respect. This was a great lady, not a glorified photo op. Suddenly, visibly moved, he knelt down next to her, gently brushing back an errant lock of her white hair from her eyes, pressing his face close to hers.

At that moment, Zoe clicked. And then she shot off a series as she held her breath.

Kate blinked from all the attention. Something was bothering her and she frowned, trying to pluck it from her brain. Suddenly, she turned to Teddy.

"Are you leaving?" she asked, searching his eyes.

Teddy stroked her face gently. Judith's words reverberated in his brain. "You need to remember who you are, where your allegiances lie." Looking up at Liza, then at Zoe, and again at his mother, something seemed to settle within him. He was surprised to find the answer waiting. Much more, he knew with a certainty it was right. He kissed his mother on the top of her head.

"Let's step out back, Judith," he said. "The view is spectacular and we need to talk."

Standing out on the lawn overlooking the ocean, watching the last vestiges of the day's light fading, Teddy turned to his campaign manager. "You have been amazing. I know you know that, so I won't belabor the point." He grinned. "I'm really so grateful to you, for everything."

"Teddy," Judith said. "You're probably *doing* this woman you've found on the island and it doesn't matter. This Liza. I'm not mad. It doesn't mean anything. But playtime's over. Now, I've got reservations on the last plane out of here. We'll get back to California and I am going to run you up and down the state like a—"

"I'm dropping out of the race."

It took a moment for his declaration to register, though somewhere deep down she had partly expected it. "You do this and the party will wash its hands of you," Judith said. "You know that, right?"

"Maybe," Teddy answered calmly. "But right now there are people who need me and, for once, I have to be here for them."

Judith eyed him in silence.

"I'll phone the party heads," Teddy assured her, "contact the campaign workers. Explain it's about family and that you had nothing to do with it."

"If you think they're going to understand or forgive you, you're sadly mistaken," Judith responded bitterly, staring hard at him. "Ironic, isn't it?" she noted icily. "We only wanted to raise your family values numbers."

A seagull flew down and propped himself on the gate in front of them.

Teddy embraced her gently, with heartfelt emotion. "Thank you, Judith," he said. "I mean it, for everything. If not for you, I would never have come here."

She shook her head. "You picked a hell of a time to grow a conscience," she muttered.

Moments later, Judith said a brusque farewell to everyone inside and Teddy announced he would be back at the house shortly. He needed to get his *former* campaign manager out on the last flight of the day.

Liza and Zoe exchanged surprised glances. Something was up and they couldn't wait to hear the details.

A short time later Teddy stood with Judith outside the entrance to Nantucket's airport. Silently, they eyed each other.

"You're going to land on your feet," Teddy said.

"Don't worry about me," Judith replied stoically. "I can do a lot of things."

"Don't I know it," Teddy said with a small grin. "You're the original multitasker."

Judith headed for the terminal then paused, turning back. "You're going to regret this, you know," she called out.

"I have a lot of regrets," Teddy responded, nodding with conviction. "This won't be one of them."

45

It was dark when Teddy returned from the airport. The blackness seemed to envelop him. His mother had told him to never give up on what you love, hadn't she? He needed more time with her. If that was selfish, then damn it, he felt like being selfish.

Before entering the house, Teddy paused outside to place a few phone calls he knew needed to be made. One was to leave word with the governor of California, apologizing for his decision to drop out of the race and explaining the circumstances of his mother's condition and his responsibility to be by her side. He thanked the governor for his support and wished the party well in the upcoming primary and fall election, promising to help if he could on his return. He made similar calls to several of his biggest supporters and phoned his headquarters, asking forgiveness and understanding for his sudden decision to quit the campaign, noting that it was something he had to do for his family and thanking them for their incredible efforts on his behalf.

Teddy next left word for Joanna about their mother's condition and then put in a call to Miranda. His ex-wife was utterly amazed.

"I don't know how to respond," Miranda said. "You encourage our daughter to discover her talent. Now you're dropping out of the race?" She paused. "I don't know what's happened to you, helping Zoe and your mother this way. I can't believe I'm saying this to you but—I admire you for it."

Her words took him by surprise. He hadn't received such grace or kindness from her in years, nor had he displayed any toward her.

"Thanks," he said. "That means a lot to me." And he was sincere.

Turning to make his way up the steps, he met Frank coming out. The older man appeared ashen.

"What is it, Frank? You look awful."

Frank took out a handkerchief and wiped his brow.

"Your mother," he explained, shaking his head. "She asked me again . . . she wants me to—" He broke off, unable to speak the words.

"She asked you to help her take a swim?" Teddy prodded.

Frank opened his mouth, surprised. "Yes . . . ," he said slowly. He stared at Teddy. "I told her I can't. I just can't, Teddy," he insisted.

Teddy put his hands on the older man's shoulders. "It's all right, Frank," he said soothingly, with a sad smile. "It's all right."

When Frank had driven off, Teddy rejoined Liza and Zoe, and together they helped Kate to bed.

"I had a great day, Grandma," Zoe said, kissing the older woman on the cheek after she tucked her in. "Thanks for being an artist."

Touched, Teddy bent down and kissed Kate on the forehead, too. "Good night, Mom. Thanks for being an artist."

Kate gazed up into his eyes, recognizing him. "Swim?" she asked plaintively.

Teddy swallowed hard. "You just get some rest, Mom," he whispered. He winced as she coughed, her voice growing raspier. Gently stroking her hand, he turned off the light.

Liza cleaned up downstairs while Teddy and Zoe talked in her room. He told her of his decision to leave the campaign.

"Are you okay, Dad?" Zoe asked, searching his eyes.

Teddy took a deep breath and held her gaze. "Yeah," he said. "I bet I was the proudest father in that gallery today. Good for you, Zoe," he said, kissing her forehead. "Good for you." He put his arm around her, not sure if he should raise the topic but afraid not to. "I hope you're not going to hurt yourself anymore, but we still need to get some help. You know that, right?"

Zoe was silent and glanced over at one of her photographs leaning against the wall.

"It's going to be all right," Teddy said, giving her a hug before getting up to leave. And then he turned back. "I love you, Zoe. I'm not sure you really believe that. But you will."

Coming back downstairs, he found Liza in the art studio, staring at his mother's work.

"Hi there," he greeted her.

"Hey." She smiled, then looked twice at his face. "You dropped out of the race," she said.

Her remark both surprised him and didn't. He hadn't told her yet, not in so many words, and still she knew. He nodded.

"That woman," Liza probed teasingly. "Judith. You and she . . ." She raised her eyebrows suggestively, waiting.

"Yeah." Teddy shrugged. "There was a physical connection, but that's all it was, for both of us." He looked into her eyes. "It wasn't real, you know?"

She walked over and enveloped him in her arms.

Teddy closed his eyes and held on tightly. The weight of all that had happened seemed to pour into that embrace. Slowly, he opened his eyes and found he was facing his mother's completed work sitting on the easel, bathed in the moonlight pouring through the windows. He led Liza over to it, and their eyes wandered over the canvas that was filled with ocean and figures and harmony. Standing there now, Teddy was struck anew by how his mother's two styles had blended into one, as if this were what she'd always had in mind.

Liza was drawn to Kate's depiction of the sea. As the moonlight picked up the brushstrokes of color, the water seemed to undulate before her.

"Your mother has such a gift. I was looking at some of her other work before you came in. And then I found these," she said, pulling him over to a table where she had laid out three small paintings.

"Where did you find them?" Teddy asked.

"I'm a bit of a snoop," Liza admitted with a shrug. "I was opening up a few drawers to see what your mother kept in her studio and there they were, wrapped in cloth."

"She kept these?" Teddy whispered.

"Of course," Liza answered. "They're by her son and they're amazing."

Teddy studied the work from his childhood. One painting was a crude watercolor of the beach below the house. The second depicted a series of bluefish he and Frank had caught off Tuckernuck Island. The third was of a woman diving into the ocean. She was surrounded by starfish and dolphins and seemed one with the sea.

Turning them over, Teddy saw where his mother had noted his age—*Teddy, age 7,* read the first one. The second had been completed the next year. The final one of his mother had been painted when Teddy was just nine and a half. He held this last painting out before him, trying to reimagine what it had felt like to wield the brush at such a tender age. Suddenly, he began to tremble at the beauty of it, as if he'd been separated from one of his limbs, torn from a thing he'd once loved, and now, tantalizingly, it could be his again.

Liza stood beside him, her eyes moving from the painting in Teddy's hand to the emotions playing out on his face. "So much passion for such a young boy," she said softly.

Teddy put down the painting and turned to her, taking her hand. "Stay with me awhile," he whispered.

She squeezed his hand tightly in response. And then Teddy led her from the studio, up the stairs, and out onto the widow's walk.

46

Climbing out into the Nantucket night, Teddy led Liza along the walk to the railing facing the Atlantic. She gazed out at the sparkling stars and the light they reflected shimmering on the ocean below.

"It's magnificent," she breathed as Teddy held her in his embrace.

Having picked up a blanket from the linen closet on his way outside, Teddy now drew it about them.

"I used to find my mother up here when I was a kid," he said. "She'd be gazing out at the ocean. Sometimes she'd have this strange look on her face. Like she was waiting for something," he said quietly. "Or some*one*."

Liza snuggled closer to him.

"She's a remarkable woman, your mother," Liza said. "Having the will to finish that painting." She turned to Teddy. "There's something that feeds the passion of an artist like her and it goes deeper than illness. You helped her to find it."

"It's not me. It's out there." Teddy nodded. "She used to say the ocean talked to her." He grinned, slightly embarrassed. "I guess I think sometimes it talks to me, too."

Liza smiled. "Really?" She studied him. "What's it telling you now?"

Teddy looked out over the water, searching, waiting.

Liza was impressed by his powers of concentration. There was something almost childlike about him as he inclined his ear, straining to listen, to hear. It seemed to her that the heaviness and worry she'd seen in him the last few days were falling away. In their place were innocence and a deep intuition, as if he were reclaiming himself.

"It's telling me something I'm supposed to know," he began softly. His eyes searched the dark waters illuminated by the gold of the summer moon. "That you can leave a place, but it never leaves you. That no matter how bad things get, how hurt you might feel, the truth heals and it leads you back to what—and who—you love."

Listening to the sounds of the ocean, Liza allowed his words to sink in before she spoke. "When Tim went down in that plane, I couldn't go near the water," she said, her eyes on the spot where the moonlight shone on the ocean. "Not for months. Which is pretty hard 'cause we're on an *island,*" she half-joked. "It was like this huge graveyard of dreams."

Liza focused her eyes on the waves illuminated in the dark, the night air alive with the rhythmic roar of the surf. "When I finally did decide to come down to the shore, I stared out at the water for a long time. Then I took off my shoes and dipped my toes in. I thought it would feel cold and dead. I remember staring down at my feet, the water swirling around them. But it was just the opposite. There was life in it. It was then that I was first able to let go and begin to move on . . ."

Teddy gazed into her eyes. There was hope there and light. His mother used to fix her eyes on a canvas before she began to paint and call it "full of possibilities." That's what he saw in Liza's eyes. And more—a willingness to risk loving him.

" I have a confession." He grinned.

"Oh." She looked curious.

"As a boy I always wanted to get a girl up here so we could . . ." He lifted his eyebrows mischievously.

"You were a horny little guy then." She laughed.

Teddy nodded. "Always." His smile vanished as his heart picked up speed. He gazed into her eyes, wanting her. And then, with a sudden need that surprised both of them, Teddy pulled her to him, his mouth hungrily finding hers. He kissed her chin, her cheeks, her forehead, his lips moving languorously over her skin. It was a delicate, caring caress that caused a warmth to surge up within Liza as she held him tightly. She buried her face in his neck with gasps of pleasure, her hands stroking his back, his face, his legs, as if she couldn't get enough of him.

Atop the thin blanket they removed each other's clothes, body falling softly into body. It felt to each of them as if they were newly discovering the ability to make love. They strained to get closer, skin rubbing skin, releasing muffled cries into the soft ocean breeze. Deep desires that had been pent up inside, untapped and unrealized, were given their due. Their cries of passion, when they climaxed, freed a burden each had carried. Lying spent against each other, they were naked and vibrant, like colors splashed against the darkness of the night. They lay looking up at the canopy of stars overhead, listening to their ragged breathing, lost in the infinite possibility of it all.

"Can you stay the night with me?" Teddy asked, his arms embracing her, not wanting to let her go.

Liza turned to him, cuddling in his arms. "I don't think that would be fair to Zoe," she said softly.

"Right," Teddy agreed reluctantly. "Not yet. But soon."

"I'm going to hold you to that," Liza said with a cute grin that made Teddy's heart ache.

He turned and kissed her gently on her eyelids. "I just want to stop time for a while," he said. "I need to hold on to this, all of it, Zoe, Kate, you. I've only just begun to know my mother and I'm going to have to let her go—I want to slow it down, at least her ultimate departure."

Liza held him close. "Time is like the ocean," she said. "It doesn't stop. Love can be like that, I think." She placed her hand gently on his heart. "It's the love you're feeling right now that you can hold on to forever." She paused, studying his face. "You have an artist's soul. You really are your mother's son," she said, kissing him gently.

Gazing out at the sea below, Teddy could feel her hand above his beating heart, its life force in sync with hers. Liza's words, her touch, unlocked something within him and he nodded. She was right. He couldn't slow down or stop what was happening to his mother, but he could love her and the others in his life with a passion he'd learned from Kate.

Reaching out, he pulled Liza close to him once more and together they listened to the ebb and flow of the waves below.

"Do you think you'd ever want to run for office again?"

"I don't know," Teddy murmured. "Maybe . . ."

"I think you'd be good," she said softly. "I have a feeling you'd be a whole different candidate now."

He raised his eyebrows, questioning.

"That's a compliment." She grinned.

Later, after they had dressed, Teddy walked Liza out, giving her the keys to his car.

"I'll pick up Zoe for you in the morning," she said. "Your phone's going to be ringing when the news of your dropping out of the race gets out. Try to get some rest."

"Yeah, you're right, thanks," Teddy replied as she got into the convertible and pulled out of the driveway.

He turned his attention to the lighthouse next door. The memory of trying to climb to the top of the structure when he was a boy rushed to the surface. His mother had warned him many times of the danger and yet he had chosen to ignore her. The spectacular fall and broken leg he suffered then had made him fear heights ever since. He wished she was well enough to counsel him now. He had decided on his own to drop out of the race, and now he was swimming in uncharted waters. Teddy looked back at the house and his mother's window on the second floor. He'd never operated without a plan in his adult life. There was no job waiting for him, no one hanging on his every word. He was just a man with a mother who was dying. He couldn't help but think of how many other sons and daughters, grandchildren and spouses were going through the same agony right that minute elsewhere in the world.

Teddy made his way around the house to make sure the gate to the beach was firmly locked. Entering the house, he checked in on Zoe and his mother. Both were sleeping. Back in his room, he saw that his cell phone showed eleven messages and his Black-Berry reported a flurry of e-mails received. It had already started, he groaned, leaving them for the morning.

As he lay his head down on the pillow, his mind wandered back to the childhood paintings Liza had discovered. He especially remembered finishing the last one of his mother diving into the water. With that image in his mind, an exhausted Teddy surrendered to sleep.

47

Teddy rose at dawn and sat for a few minutes at the edge of his bed. He'd slept fitfully, his mind filled with calls he needed to make and people he would have to reach out to. He had listened to his mother's labored breathing when he checked in on her before retiring, and he planned to speak to Dr. Jennings today. Despite her wishes not to take any medicine for infections, Teddy hoped to see if there was at least something, anything, the doctor could give her that might help. Getting up, he pulled on shorts and a sweatshirt and headed down the hallway to look in on Kate.

Gently pushing open the door, Teddy found the bed empty. He stepped in and saw that the bathroom door was closed.

"Mom, you all right?" he called out.

There was no answer. Teddy knocked lightly.

"Mom? Kate?"

Teddy turned the doorknob and pushed open the door. There was no one in the room. "What the . . . ?" he blurted out, shaking his head as he turned around and headed out into the hallway. The large wicker chair he had used to block the passage up to the roof was still in place. He looked in Zoe's room, finding her alone and sleeping. He hurried down the stairs, fortified by the thought that in addition to blocking the way to the roof the night before, he had made certain the gate down to the beach was locked. He ran to the kitchen and found it empty. Then he rushed to the art studio. No sign of her. As panic set in, Teddy raced out to the back lawn. As he scrambled toward the gate, he could see it was closed. Thank God. But where could Kate have gone?

Teddy gave the gate a hearty shake. It was sturdy and locked, just as he had left it. But as he stood there looking down he found something he'd not taken notice of before. The crossboards in the middle were loose. He reached down and pushed on them. As he did, they split open, leaving a hole in the center of the white-slatted barrier. When he pulled his hand away, the crossboards swung back into place. Teddy's heart began to pound as fear engulfed him. Was it possible his mother was so determined to take that swim, so fierce of mind even in her frail condition, that finding a barrier she couldn't remove she had discovered a way to simply go through it?

Unlocking the gate, Teddy ran down the pathway, his feet bare, fear gripping him. Would he find her again sitting on the red boat or could she have . . . ? As he barreled down the slope, above the tall grass and shrubbery, the beach came into view. Teddy didn't pause for a minute as he ran ahead, his eyes scanning left and right.

And then he saw her. She was standing at the shoreline.

"Kate?" he called out. "Kate!" Teddy's heart was in his throat. "Mom," he screamed as he spilled out onto the beach, falling hard to the sand. Picking himself up, he saw his mother, dressed in her nightgown, the hem reaching into the water, begin to walk briskly into the ocean. She was a hundred feet ahead as Teddy ran, his heart threatening to explode through his chest.

"Mom? Mom? It's me," Teddy yelled out. "I'm coming. Stop!"

But Kate continued to wade deep into the water, oblivious to his cries. Teddy knifed through the sand, squinting in the bright sunlight of an eastern sky. All he could think of was that his mother must not die out there. He had to reach her. And then he was in the ocean, his legs kicking through the morning tide, his eyes glued on Kate some thirty feet ahead, waist high in water.

Suddenly, something within Teddy grabbed hold of him and he came to a stop.

He stared at his mother as she walked farther into the water. His logical mind told his feet to move forward, but another voice kept him still. This was her way of letting go, wasn't it? Here she was, making the choice she had spoken of to Frank. She had been trying to get down to the ocean for this last swim, and everyone had prevented it, the same way they had all stood in the way of her painting. He himself had risked taking her in the boat but had refused to allow her to get in the water. Yet she had found a way. The stubbornness, the tenacity he admired in her was even stronger than this cursed illness.

In grief, Teddy looked on as the morning sun rose, its golden rays dappling the waves. His mother's body seemed to glow as she moved slowly forward, her mind plagued with illness, but her spirit undaunted, unbowed. She was *choosing* to end her life in the ocean she loved, of this he was certain. He gazed at her, his throat tight with emotion, his mind oddly calm. If he let her go now, she would be at peace. The landscape he watched was like some Impressionist painting in which the light seemed embedded in the paint. But this was real, too, all too real.

The water had reached her shoulders. Only her head bobbed above the gentle waves. She seemed to pause, then, looking around.

Was she disoriented? Teddy's mind rebelled again. It was quite possible she didn't really know what she was doing, wasn't it? How could she know, in her state?

No, he told himself, once again resigned. If she had somehow managed to overcome the physical barriers placed in front of her, not to mention the limitations of her body and brain due to her condition, then this was truly her choice. It was coming from someplace the disease couldn't touch or hadn't yet destroyed. It wasn't right to hold on to her, to control her. This was her will and he must honor it. His feet tingled in the cold waters and he began to shiver. What was his mother feeling now?

She was fifty, sixty feet away from him. Temporarily blinded as light reflected off the ocean, Teddy shielded his eyes and strained to find her. His mind panicked. God, had he lost her already? He moved a few steps forward into the surf. There was a pounding at his temples. And then Teddy found her again. The sunlight bathed her in its brilliance. He could barely discern her figure from the ocean now. But a slight movement, bouncing upward, caught his eye, and he saw her clearly again. Kate was pushing off of the ocean floor. And then, in a fluid gesture, she was swimming. Teddy's heart leapt into his throat, his mind pleading with him to go to her. But something stronger held him back. He was not in control. *She* was. And that, he knew somewhere deep beneath his shivering skin, was as it should be. She swam harder and farther out than he would ever have thought possible.

He was unsure how long he'd been watching her. For Teddy, time had stopped. And then, in the blink of an eye, he saw his mother's head arch back and slip into the water. She seemed to melt into the ocean, as if taking new form. The light shone bright where she swam and then, like the softest of brushstrokes, Kate Mathison was gone.

At that moment, as the tide lapped at his ankles, Teddy felt a dam of emotion break free within him. And there, alone, in the sunlit dappled waters of dawn, he sobbed for his mother, for his father, for all that had been needlessly lost. He cried for opportunities squandered, for love unrealized and relationships betrayed. But his heart wouldn't stop there. He felt a wave of thankfulness for Joanna's having called him to the island, for the chance to know his mother before she was gone. He cried with appreciation for the gift of Kate's art and her love.

Because of *her*, he was rekindling his relationship with his daughter. Because of *her*, he was opening himself to Liza, learning to love not as a boy, but as a man. Teddy breathed through his tears. He opened his eyes and took in the powerful forces of ocean and dawn. Time ceased. There was only this moment. He felt a fullness rise within him, and turning his face to the sun, Teddy finally *let go.*

Before he knew it, he, too, was swimming. The ocean washed away his tears as he made his way to the spot where his mother had blended into the sea. He searched the area, diving below the surface, desperate to locate her before her body could be carried off in the strong currents that ringed the island. And then, coming up for air, he felt her a few feet below the surface, lifeless. He dove back down, placing his arms around her frail body, and held her tightly to his chest as he ascended. Cradling her, he allowed his eyes to wander across her face, those eyes that had once found beauty and put it on canvas. He lifted her limp hands, hands that had wielded a brush with magic. He turned and, using the skills he had learned on the island so many summers ago, gently pulled her back to shore.

Emerging from the ocean, Teddy held his mother in his arms and carried her over to the red boat sitting on its side. Laying her gently against it, he knelt down, combing her hair with his fingers. Waves crashed on shore as he said good-bye to his mother. He could see that the soul of her, the light, was missing, but he also knew it was elsewhere now, part of a larger canvas.

Bending over, he kissed her on the forehead. "I love you, Mom," he said softly. "Thank you . . . for everything."

Epilogue

September. Fall was making its crisp appearance on the island as Liza greeted Teddy with a forceful embrace at the small airport. They held each other for a long time and then, arms intertwined, walked back to her car. Teddy had come to close up the old house for the winter. But he planned to stay for at least a month, seeing to some odds and ends before returning to L.A. To his delight, Liza had agreed to come back with him to California for a visit. He looked forward to giving her a tour of the coast. He couldn't be sure how things would proceed, or if their relationship could weather their living on different coasts. For now, though, it was enough to have her in his life. For this, he was grateful beyond words.

Zoe had started at her new school and apparently decided to give it a chance. He and Miranda were dealing with the aftermath of Zoe's emotional problems. Teddy hoped his daughter would put it all behind her and never hurt herself again, but he couldn't be sure. Yet, for the first time, he had the feeling Zoe was growing into who she was meant to be. There would be other rough times between them, and he couldn't erase the past, but they had forged a new relationship on the island, and he would make certain that it grew and flourished.

As Liza drove him to Sconset from the airport, Teddy caught sight of the lighthouse and the ocean and thought of his mother. They had sprinkled Kate's ashes off the bow of Frank's sailboat a few days after she had gone for her last swim. The Irishman had never asked him for the details of what had happened that morning, but when their eyes first met, Teddy saw gratitude there. Joanna had had the same reaction when she'd arrived for the funeral, holding Teddy tightly and, without words, thanking him for having been there for their mother.

Despite the jaded view of Teddy's former campaign manager when it came to him and relationships, he had discovered that he liked being bound to something and to someone. He had also learned that "letting go" was not the same as "giving up." Far from it.

Now, as Liza prepared a welcome-home dinner in the kitchen of the summerhouse, Teddy gathered supplies from the art studio and made his way out back. "Never give up on who or what you love," his mother had said. He breathed in the salty air and stared out at the ocean. Taking hold of a white canvas, he placed it on an easel and grasped a palette. Squeezing out the contents of several tubes, Teddy dabbed the canvas with some magenta, some yellow, and something "bluer than blue." He reached for his paintbrush. Scanning the waters before him, he listened intently.

"Paint me a picture, Teddy," he heard his mother say. "Paint me a picture of what you see."

Lifting his brush, he dipped it in the colors on the palette. He gazed once more out at the silvery blue waters being buffeted by an autumn wind. Teddy smiled. Taking a deep breath, he began.

About the Author

Jan Goldstein's debut novel, *All That Matters,* was a selection of the Literary Guild, the Doubleday Book Club, the Book-of-the-Mouth Club, and the Quality Paperback Club. An *L.A. Times* bestseller, the novel has been translated into numerous languages, including Japanese, Thai, Portuguese, Spanish, Chinese, Polish, and Greek. He is currently at work on the screenplay. He is the father of five and lives in Los Angeles with his wife, Bonnie, and their family. Visit his website at www.JanGoldstein.com.

Discussion Questions for
The Prince of Nantucket

1. At the opening of the novel, Judith tells Teddy that he isn't made for relationships. What do we learn about him early on that would give this statement validity?

2. How does Zoe view her father? What do you feel adolescent girls want most in a father?

3. At the Even Keel Cafe on Nantucket, Zoe sets up rules for Teddy regarding women. What are they? What do these rules say, if anything, about how Zoe might want to be treated?

4. Teddy blames his mother for some terrible act that altered his life. And yet it gradually becomes evident that he admires her for several traits. What are they and why are they important to Teddy?

5. We come to see that the old family friend and caretaker, Frank, has an unrequited love. What advice does this cause him to give Teddy? There are other characters in the novel who possess love that has gone unrequited, as well as parts of themselves that have gone unfulfilled. Identify them and discuss what those unrequited or unfulfilled aspects are for each character.

6. How does Zoe express her pain? What other ways do people, young and old, express or bury that in life which hurts them the most?

7. Why do you feel the author set this story on an island? Are there other kinds of islands in this novel?

8. Within this story, art plays a major role in healing and expressing one's identity. The author's own mother was a poet who, at the end of her life, suffered from Alzheimer's. He has said that he and other family members were able to communicate with her through the use of poetry. What was there about art that allowed Teddy to "unlock" Kate's memory? Do you feel art, and other forms of creative expression, might unlock parts of ourselves we don't normally reach? Discuss how this could be applied to your life or the lives of those you love.

9. Kate initially becomes frustrated, in once again, trying to paint under Teddy's guidance. What does her "handprint" signify to her and to Teddy? Imagine you are Teddy watching his mother paint again. Describe your emotions.

10. What does Liza, who has experienced tragedy, say one must do with that pain in order to move on? Discuss the ways in which you or those you love have moved through difficult or tragic times. What or who helped you? What do you do with the pain?

11. Zoe takes a photograph that stuns Teddy when Liza shows it to him. What was the subject of the photo and what did it tell Teddy about the way his daughter sees herself?

12. Clearly, Zoe was keeping a secret from her parents. Would your child or grandchild be able to keep such a secret from you? What do we hide from those we love and why do we do it?

13. Gradually, the importance of the campaign back in California diminishes in Teddy's eyes, replaced by concerns about the three women he is dealing with on Nantucket. Discuss how each of these female characters alters him in some way. Are there women (or men) who have changed the way in which you see yourself and the world?

14. Why did Kate keep such a secret from Teddy? How did learning the truth change his view of his father and mother? How does he create a second chance for him and his mother? Discuss the importance of second chances in your own life and in the lives of those you are close to.

15. Do you agree with Liza's assessment that the Teddy we come to know at the end of the story would make a very different candidate should he ever decide to run again? How so?

16. The author has said he wanted to depict a character "rediscovering the artist in himself." Do you believe there is an artist (however you interpret that) inside each of us?

17. What emotions does Kate's final request of her son generate in you? How would you have responded?

18. Discuss Teddy's decision in regard to his mother's stunning last request and contrast his willingness to give up control and allow his mother her own choice. What is the author saying about love in this final act?